Berkley Books by Ally Carter

CHEATING AT SOLITAIRE

LEARNING TO PLAY GIN

Learning to Play Gin

Ally Carter

BERKLEY BOOKS, NEW YORK

THE BERKLEY PUBLISHING GROUP
Published by the Penguin Group
Penguin Group (USA) Inc.
375 Hudson Street, New York, New York 10014, USA
Penguin Group (Canada), 90 Eglinton Avenue East, Suite 700, Toronto, Ontario M4P 2Y3, Canada
(a division of Pearson Penguin Canada Inc.)
Penguin Books Ltd., 80 Strand, London WC2R 0RL, England
Penguin Group Ireland, 25 St. Stephen's Green, Dublin 2, Ireland (a division of Penguin Books Ltd.)
Penguin Group (Australia), 250 Camberwell Road, Camberwell, Victoria 3124, Australia
(a division of Pearson Australia Group Pty. Ltd.)
Penguin Books India Pvt. Ltd., 11 Community Centre, Panchsheel Park, New Delhi—110 017, India
Penguin Group (NZ), Cnr. Airborne and Rosedale Roads, Albany, Auckland 1310, New Zealand
(a division of Pearson New Zealand Ltd.)
Penguin Books (South Africa) (Pty.) Ltd., 24 Sturdee Avenue, Rosebank, Johannesburg 2196, South Africa

Penguin Books Ltd., Registered Offices: 80 Strand, London WC2R 0RL, England

This book is an original publication of The Berkley Publishing Group.

This is a work of fiction. Names, characters, places, and incidents either are the product of the author's imagination or are used fictitiously, and any resemblance to actual persons, living or dead, business establishments, events, or locales is entirely coincidental. The publisher does not have any control over and does not assume any responsibility for author or third-party websites or their content.

First edition: November 2006

Library of Congress Cataloging-in-Publication Data

Carter, Ally.
  Learning to play gin / Ally Carter.— 1st ed.
    p. cm.
  ISBN 0-425-21192-4 (trade pbk.)
  1. Single women—Fiction. 2. Women authors—Fiction. 3. Chick lit. I. Title.

PS3603.A7765L43 2006
813'.6—dc22
                                2006025861

PRINTED IN THE UNITED STATES OF AMERICA

10 9 8 7 6 5 4 3 2 1

For Mom, my first and greatest teacher

Acknowledgments

No book happens without the help of dozens of people, and this one is far from the exception. I am forever grateful to the amazing Kate Seaver, who opened my eyes to what this book could be, and Kristin Nelson, who kept me going.

Also, thanks go out to Heidi Mack, Jana DeLeon, Susan Willis, Gay Barker, and Connie Woodard and everyone at Berkley whose help and support kept me sane.

And finally I thank my friends and family, whom I love.

Prologue

ARE THEY OR AREN'T THEY?

June 12, New York—Two months ago, mega-author Julia James had written the book on how to be single—literally. Her three international bestsellers were the must-have accessory of single women everywhere, but then in the shot heard round the world, women got a wakeup call—their role model had a boyfriend.

Or did she? Rumors and innuendo followed James and then out-of-work actor Lance Collins for two weeks, ending in an unequivocal denial of a relationship by Collins in an interview in the April edition of *FAD* magazine. Just weeks following that announcement, however, representatives from the James camp confirmed that the author and the actor were, in fact, an item, legitimizing the rumors that the most famously single woman in the world had found herself a man.

Collins and James have each been photographed separately since—she near her home in Oklahoma and he on location at film sets in New York and New Zealand, but not since they were initially photographed on the streets of New York have they been seen together. In fact, no photographic evidence of their relationship exists since the monumental success of her book, *101 Ways to Cheat at Solitaire,* and his climb from obscurity, leaving many industry insiders to wonder if this really was a case of love at first sight or just the greatest PR ploy of all time.

In this town—that's saying something.

Chapter One

Gin is a game most people learn in two phases. They may learn the basic rules in a few minutes. The finer points may take months or even years. Others, unfortunately, will never master the game.

Julia looked at the cards in her hand. They were her cards, Hoyle brand—red and black, faded and scuffed so unmistakably that no one would play her in poker because she knew what everyone else was holding. It was something she'd grown used to—being able to call bluffs.

The marks on those cards were her marks. Their creases were her lines—wrinkles that told of far too many sleepless nights and games of solitaire. They were the indentations of a woman who, no matter the game, had grown too used to cheating.

But for all the times Julia had sat on that same bed, looking at those same cards, she'd never been so confused. But then again, over the course of the past nine months, all the rules had changed.

And she was no longer on that bed alone.

"Just play one already!" Nina snapped.

Julia looked at her best friend. Her promise to give up solitaire for gin was supposed to come with instructions from a six-foot-two-inch movie star. What she got instead was a five-one interior decorator. It was just one of many ways the game had stumped her.

Julia pulled a card randomly from her hand and laid it faceup on the discard pile. She looked at Nina and wondered, not for the first time, if she was doing the right thing—if that six of diamonds would someday come back to haunt her.

She started to ask, but ever since the night when Nina showed up, distraught because the man she'd married and divorced twice was getting married again (just not to her this time), Julia had felt like she had to be careful around Nina. It was a new phenomenon. The Nina she'd known her whole life had been brazen and bold and beyond mortality—nothing but a series of crazy stories that would somehow live forever in her indestructible wake. Now, Nina was different, so Julia didn't look at her—didn't ask. She just wished she could have her six of diamonds back.

"Humph-hum." Nina cleared her throat loudly, jolting Julia. "It's your turn again," Nina said, half-teasing.

But Julia just looked back down at the bed at Nina's queen of hearts and wondered, *What's that supposed to mean?* It was the writer in her. Everything was supposed to be symbolic. Was this Nina's way of saying she was over her ex-husband—that she was moving into the next phase of her life—the non-Jason, non-men, happily independent phase? Julia started to ask, but then Nina said, "Do you think Eduardo is hot?" She rearranged her cards a little. "I think Eduardo's hot," and Julia got her answer.

Eduardo *was* hot, Julia presumed, in the way Italian mosaic artists are supposed to be—dark and tortured and a little on the hairy side. She imagined that he'd make women fall in love and then break them like pieces of tile so that he could put them back together in his own special way. Nina, Julia feared, was already a little bit broken.

So Julia said, "Sure, Eduardo is hot, but he is also going to finish that ridiculously expensive foyer in a few days and then he's going back to Italy."

But Nina didn't reply. She just kept rearranging the cards in her hands, probably not by any logical order, probably so that they looked the prettiest, and Julia realized that Nina was the kind of girl who was always putting the queen of hearts out there. Julia was the kind of girl who was always holding it in.

♣

Lately, there were a lot of things Lance Collins couldn't get used to, like having a suite at the Ritz where hair and makeup people banged on his door, like having jet lag so bad he wasn't sure if the digital clock was telling him that it was four-thirty in the morning or afternoon, like having the doorman look at him as if he were thinking, *So that's Lance Collins—he's shorter than he looks on TV.*

But as Lance stepped out onto the sidewalk into the chill of the autumn air, a uniformed driver reached for the rear door of a shiny black sedan and said, "Good morning, Mr. Collins. My name's Charlie, and I'll be taking you to—"

"Rockefeller Center. We know. We know." A woman pushed Lance to the far side of the car and glared up at the man holding the door. "Just drive, please."

That was the thing Lance was having the hardest time getting used to—the fact that in this world there were professional gripers/ whiners/complainers/sender-backers/yellers/screamers/and/"do you know who this is"-ers. They were all too thin, too wired, and too caffeinated, and for a fee, they could be yours on a temporary basis. This one pulled an enormous black leather tote in after her, adjusted the grip on the cell phone she clutched beneath her chin, took a swig from her Starbucks cup, then whispered, "I *hate* chatty drivers." She shifted the phone to her shoulder and patted his lapel. "Yes, I'm with him right now, and he looks fabulous!"

"Thank you," Lance said to the driver as soon as the

woman had turned back to her phone. He wasn't sure how having a professional handler was supposed to save him any time if he spent so much energy quietly apologizing for them. He looked at the woman beside him and tried to remember her name. Was it Kayla? No. Kayla had been his handler in London. Maybe Kylie? Maybe Kim? *It doesn't matter,* he decided finally, resting his head back, feeling his body sink into a sleepless trance, *there'll be another one tomorrow.*

He might have dozed off if Kayla-Kylie-Kim hadn't cried out at regular intervals, "I know!" and "So right!" and finally, "That's what *I* keep telling him." She eyed Lance and winked. "Did you know he got off the plane by himself last night? It was the sweetest thing I've ever seen. He doesn't even know he's a big star." Kayla-Kylie-Kim's cell phone was back against her shoulder, muffling her acidic voice against the intrusive ears of the person on the other end of the line. "Darling, you simply *have* to get yourself an entourage."

Lance didn't want an entourage. He wanted a bed, but he probably wasn't going to see one anytime soon, because just as Lance closed his eyes, Kayla-Kylie-Kim shot forward and started digging in her bag. "Oh no, I've already talked to Stephanie at Paramount and . . ."

She kept talking, but Lance didn't hear her. He looked through the window at the weather, expecting spring but seeing fall. A season was missing, so after five months south of the equator, he had to wonder why summer had neither come nor gone.

"I say, Mr. Collins," Charlie said, and Lance leaned toward the driver. Beside him Kayla-Kylie-Kim was shouting about fruit trays and bottled water, but the driver's voice was calm and even, as if he'd heard it all before. "Could I ask you how Miss James is doing?"

At the mention of Julia's name, Kayla-Kylie-Kim dropped her cell phone and snapped, "Mr. Collins will not be answering questions regarding—"

Lance saw the driver's eyes narrow in the rearview mirror, so he held a hand out to stop her.

"Oh, I'm sorry, sir," the man rushed to say. "I didn't mean . . . It's just . . . I drive her, you know? When she comes to town to promote her books. I've been driving her for years. She's a fine woman—a real fine woman—and I was hoping you might tell her I'm looking forward to driving her again."

"*He could sell this story to the tabloids,*" Kayla-Kylie-Kim warned beneath her breath, but Lance said, "She's great, Charlie. And I'll tell her you asked."

"Thank you, sir. That'd be real nice of you," Charlie beamed. "She sure is a fine lady."

Lance sighed, remembering. "That she is."

Kayla-Kylie-Kim went back to banging on her PDA and

talking on her phone, and Charlie's eyes returned to the city streets, leaving Lance to stare through the car windows at the day that was dawning on the city he used to know.

A man strolled down the sidewalk. Lance recognized the tired gait of a bartender ending his shift. He remembered how it felt to trek home with aching feet and beer-soaked clothes through those same filtered rays of sunlight.

A woman in a trim navy suit was walking in the opposite direction. Lance watched them cross paths—saw the changing of the guard in the city that never sleeps—and felt like he was seeing New York City from the wrong side of 5 a.m.

Sometimes Julia thought she spent every morning of her new life wondering where her old life had gone. Then she remembered. It had been hauled away in dump trucks; chipped away with jackhammers; sanded, polished, and painted until nothing remained but the dust and the plastic and the smell of drying plaster. In short, her life was being remodeled, one room at a time.

She stood at the top of the stairs and looked down at the foyer and living room below, listened to the hammering and sawing that floated through the plastic barrier, and thought of a title for a new book: *So You Want to Buy an Old House: Stupid Things Single Girls Do*. But then Julia caught herself. She remembered that she had retired from the nonfiction business—that, if you wanted to be really technical about it, she wasn't even single. Not really.

When Nina appeared at the base of the stairs then, arms outstretched, fabric samples dangling across her thin frame as if she were a human drapery rod, she snapped, "Get down here. It's time to pick curtains. You've got to feel me."

Julia took a step. "I thought that was Eduardo's job."

"Like he wasn't my first choice," Nina shot back. "Oh, but speaking of which . . ."

She grabbed Julia's hand and dragged her toward the foyer.

"Nina," Julia protested. "Lance is gonna be on in a—"

"We have time for this," Nina said as she fingered a sheet that had been tacked over the arching doorframe.

"Nina, I haven't even set the DVR, let me—"

"Wait," Nina said. She brought her hands together. She took a deep breath, and her voice was full of fireworks when she said, "Julia James, I give you"—*dramatic pause*—"your new foyer tile!"

With a tug, the sheet fell, and Julia looked down at a gorgeous mosaic floor that might have belonged in a European cathedral, and yet seemed perfectly at home in an Oklahoma farmhouse. It was simply beautiful and elegant and unlike anything Julia had ever dreamed of owning.

Beside her Nina giggled and bounced. "Do you want to say a few words?" Nina prompted.

"Was the sheet really necessary?"

"Hey, life's a mosaic, baby," Nina responded. "I'm not gonna let you take the grout for granted."

No, Julia realized, *you never have.*

◆

No matter how many hours Lance spent in front of a camera, he wasn't sure he'd ever get used to the feeling of being on live TV. The people at the *Today* show were pros, but the whole process ended up feeling like a barrage, of "Good morning's" and "I'm a huge fan's" and "We'll be with you in a minute's," and before Lance could get his bearings, he was in a chair in front of the perky young entertainment reporter named Karin—with an *i*—and being told to act naturally.

Ironically, that's the one kind of acting he hadn't done much of lately.

Karin was serious and professional as she spoke into the camera. "If you've picked up a magazine in the last eight months, you've seen the face of Lance Collins. Well"—she chuckled—"I for one haven't minded." Then she laughed as if she'd gone off script even though Lance could see the joke spelled out clearly on the cue card. Still, he couldn't help but blush as Karin went on.

"Heartthrob status aside, Lance Collins is one of the most in-demand young stars that Hollywood has seen in years, so it may be hard to believe that his first feature film is two weeks away from hitting theaters." She turned and beamed a smile in his direction that almost made it worth getting up at 4 a.m. "How are you, Lance? It's so great to have you here."

"I'm great, Karin. It's great to be here."

"Wow," she said, "this has been quite a year for you." Karin rested her chin in the palm of her upturned hand and asked, "Where were you a year ago?"

"From today?"

"Yes, can you remember? Or was that another lifetime entirely?" she added with a laugh.

"Oh, no, I remember. I was here." He pointed down at the island of Manhattan. "New York. Tending bar. Scraping by."

"And where were you yesterday?" she asked in the manner of someone who already knows the answer.

"London yesterday."

"And tomorrow?" Karin prompted, but Lance only grinned and shook his head, trying to cast off the fatigue and jet lag that had followed him through three continents.

"I honestly have no idea."

He laughed with that absurd realization, and before he knew it, Karin was reaching across, rubbing his arm, consoling him and laughing, too.

"Hang in there, Lance." She took a pair of dark-framed glasses and slid them onto her face then glanced down at a sheet of paper. "According to this, you are shooting a film in New Zealand right now; you have one coming out in two weeks, another coming out in February, and you have three projects lined up for next year already."

"Hey, can I have that when you're finished with it?" he asked, pointing to the cheat sheet in her hands.

"Sure," she said, laughing. "You need it more than I do!"

He sighed. "I'm not complaining. I know I'm a lucky guy."

♠

"Sorry I'm late!" Julia glanced up from the TV in time to see her sister, Caroline, come running through the front door, a purse hanging half off her arm.

The smell of paint floated through the plastic tarp that separated her hundred-year-old farmhouse from the new addition, but still Julia could smell the baby spit-up on her sister's blouse. Caroline, evidently, had grown immune.

"What?" Caroline said when she saw Julia staring. "I didn't miss it, did I? I could just kill Steve. He said he'd watch the kids this morning, but he stayed up half the night with some History Channel marathon, and then when it was time for me to leave, he—"

"No, Caroline," Julia said, "you haven't missed much."

"He's gotten hotter!" Nina said. "I didn't think it was possible, but . . ." She sighed, sank back on the plush cushions of the new couch, and said, "Yum."

Caroline pushed Nina in a *move over* gesture, and said, "Totally."

Julia looked at them both, half-irritated and half-offended because Lance was so much more than just a pretty face, but the two of them were staring at him as if he were a bull her father was trying to buy at an auction. She started to preach about objectification and inner beauty, but then she glanced back at the screen and realized, *Oh my gosh, he HAS gotten hotter!*

Then the plastic divider was swept aside. The noise from the construction got slightly louder for a split second, then dropped again as a man called, "Julia, honey, I've got to talk to—"

"Shhhh," all three women cut him off.

Sam walked softly toward the living room. "Babe, I . . ." But Sam's voice faded as he saw the screen, and he said, "Well, there's ol' Lance," proving that Sam was both the kind of man who could use the word *babe* and not sound sexist, and that when Lance had come to visit in August and worked side by side with Sam and his crew, the man had really meant it when he'd slipped Lance his business card and told him that if acting didn't work out, Lance would always have a job in construction.

The look on Sam's face was part amazement that he knew someone who was on national TV, and part disappointment because help like Lance was hard to come by.

On the screen, Karin was saying, "*Day of Days* is the

project you're working on now, isn't that right? Is it a physical role? Because I've got to say, you're looking pretty buff."

Karin reached to squeeze his bicep.

"I don't like the way she's touching him," Nina said as the anchorwoman leaned across the screen. "Do you think I could take her?" she asked Julia, who didn't dare answer, because Karin obviously worked out, but Nina fought dirty.

Still, that didn't stop Sam from saying, "I'd give you ten-to-one." Nina beamed.

"What's been the biggest change for you in the past eight months?" Karin asked, and Julia watched Lance shift in the chair.

He's nervous, she thought as Lance shrugged and said, "Well, I never dreamed I'd ever be working with this kind of material."

"Really?" Karin asked. "Come on, your dad's an Academy Award winner. You never thought you'd be where you are today?"

Lance looked down. He rubbed his palms along his jeans, and Julia glanced at Nina, Caroline, and Sam, wondering if they saw it, too, or if maybe you had to know him—to love him—to see the real answer to the question.

"Well," Lance said calmly. "Of course I always knew there were great projects out there; it's just not something I ever wanted to take for granted. So many things have to happen. So many cards have to fall into place that I never wanted to assume anything like this would happen just because of who my father happens to be."

"Is that why you don't use his last name?" Karin asked and Lance nodded.

Julia held her breath until she heard Lance say, "Sure . . . Yeah . . . That's a big part of it."

"This has got to be so amazing for you. How are you coping? Do you stay grounded?" Karin leaned closer and reasserted, "You *seem* really grounded."

"Well, Karin, there's at least one woman I can count on to keep me in line."

Julia felt her ivory cheeks turn red. She hadn't gotten used to Lance giving her compliments in private—much less on national TV. She felt a rush of giddy excitement as she threw her hands toward the screen and said, "He's not supposed to talk about me!"

Then Lance waved at the camera and said, "Hi, Mom."

Julia could feel her sister, best friend, and contractor staring holes into her.

"Well," she scoffed. "That's a relief."

"*Uh-huh,*" Nina replied with undiluted skepticism.

Karin scooted forward. "Now Lance, a little birdie told me that you recently made a very big decision and that congratulations are in order."

Congratulations? Julia honestly didn't have any idea what

Karin was talking about. Granted she hadn't seen Lance in months—but they talked or e-mailed almost daily. There was nothing congratulations-worthy.

But to her amazement, Lance said, "Yeah!" In nine months of knowing him, Julia had never seen him look more thrilled. "I bought a house! In California."

For the first time in months, Julia's house was quiet. No hammers. No saws. She just sat staring at the screen for a long time—not realizing when the interview was over—not noticing when Caroline turned off the TV.

It seemed to take an eternity for Nina to say, "Well, at least he didn't talk about you."

Chapter Two

Gin rummy is a game where a player really has to play the odds.

Julia," Caroline was saying, but Julia couldn't hear her—not really. She was too certain that her ears had stopped working. *Yeah, that explains it. My ears are on the fritz. I'm going to have to see a specialist.* She held a hand up and cupped the side of her head because she simply had to communicate with her sister somehow that she was no longer capable of hearing anything correctly. After all, she thought Lance had just told the entire *Today* show audience that he had bought a home in California, and that wasn't true—Julia would know about such a thing; he'd have told her about it, asked her advice. He knew that she was spending every minute of her time and every last ounce of her patience remodeling her old house, so her ears simply had to be on the fritz.

"He talked it over with you, didn't he?" Caroline asked, looking at her as if the reality of the situation was just starting to dawn. "He didn't talk it over with you!" Julia heard her sister exhale deeply then quickly whisper to Nina, "He didn't talk it over with her," as if bringing her up to speed on the situation.

"I wonder what kind of house it is?" Nina asked. "I bet it's Mediterranean. You know I love the Mediterranean!"

"Nina!" Caroline snapped. "You've never been to the Mediterranean."

"Well, that doesn't mean I can't appreciate architectural symmetry when I see it," Nina shot back, and Julia was amazed because this sounded like a real conversation, but it couldn't have been because the house they were talking about was Lance's, and Lance didn't own a house! *She* owned a house.

Lance had helped her decipher blueprints and pick out floor tiles. He'd walked with her through an imaginary garden, asking questions, listening with her as the landscaper said, "Now, how do you feel about azaleas? They'll take three years to mature."

Three years, Julia had thought. Three years. So much could happen.

But Lance had nodded and said, "I think that sounds good," as if he was going to stick around for that, as if waiting three years for azaleas was in his master plan. As if he was a man who could commit to shrubbery.

"I just can't believe he never talked about it with you," Caroline said, still disbelieving. "I mean, when Steve mentioned it, I—"

"Wait." Julia shot upright. "You mean, you knew about this?"

Caroline inched away, a sheepish expression on her face as she looked down at the old, oak floor and said, "Well, Steve does Lance's taxes, and he mentioned that Lance could probably use some investments to—"

"Caroline!" Julia said. "Why didn't you tell me?"

"Hey, Jules," Nina said, butting in, "do you think he's hired a decorator yet?"

"Nina," Caroline snapped, sounding very *Mom-like*, signaling that someone might need a time out.

"Oh no, what if it's already furnished?" Nina lamented, totally missing the point.

"Hey," Julia said, pushing away from her sister, turning her back on her friend. "It's great. I'm happy for him. You know he and his mom moved around all the time when he was a kid. That's something he's always said he envies about me—my roots." She gestured to the hardwood floor on which they stood—that piece of history that Lance himself had helped to sand and stain. "I'm glad he has that now. I'm . . . I'm very glad."

Then she turned, wanting to go upstairs, but she ran right into Sam.

"Oh, Sam, sorry I forgot. Was there something you—"

"It can wait!" Sam bolted for the door.

"Sam," Julia snapped, "I'm fine." Then she took a deep breath. She smiled. "Just . . . tell me what you need."

"Well," Sam said cautiously. He glanced between Nina and Caroline, waited for Caroline's nod of okay before he said, "Julia, honey, I've got good news, and I've got bad news."

"Good news," Julia blurted. "Give me the good news."

"Well . . ." Sam stumbled and stammered before finally saying, "We found a way to have the new roof match the old roof."

"Oh?" Julia said, sharing a smile with Nina. "That's really—"

But just then Julia was cut off by a terrible sound of crashing lumber and tumbling debris. She and Nina and Caroline turned and looked through the front windows as another pile of two-by-fours, shingles, and nails crashed onto the front yard. All they could do was stand there, watching the dust settle.

"The bad news is, we're gonna have to tear off the old roof."

The room seemed to be ticking—like a clock. Or a bomb. Every eye turned to Julia.

Sam rubbed his hands together. They were big and rough like him, calloused but sure, and still he couldn't look at her when he said, "We tried to save it, Julia. I swear we did. But the more we dug around up there, the worse things looked. If you want my honest opinion, it's a good thing we caught it when we did."

Julia was very familiar with Sam's honest opinion—it had told her when they pulled up the carpet in the study that she needed a whole new floor. His honest opinion had broken the news that instead of simply tapping into her existing septic tank, she was going to need a new one. It was his honest opinion that kept reminding her over and over how close everything had been to falling down around her—that if she hadn't decided to fix some things eight months before, her life would be a pile of rubble today.

"Okay," she said, taking a deep breath, forcing a smile. "Sam, really, it's okay. I'm okay. You guys just do what you have to do."

"Really?" Sam asked in the manner of a man who has delivered that same news before and gotten a *very different* reaction.

"Of course," Julia said. "It's only money." Then she remembered that was the one thing she had more than enough of.

"Oh my gosh! What time is it?" Caroline snapped as she grabbed her purse and glanced at a bare wrist that was no doubt supposed to hold a watch. She rubbed the patch of skin as if the time were printed there in Braille, then said, almost to herself, "Steve said he'd only watch the kids till nine-thirty, so he's probably either left them alone or duct-taped them into his car by now—you know he never did learn how to work the car seats."

She watched Caroline open the door and step onto the porch. She saw the winding lane she knew well enough to drive blindfolded, the distant creek, and the hills that rolled on forever. She stood there looking at them, remembering that some things never change, but then another massive section of roof fell to the yard and a flash of lightning burned across the sky and the clouds opened up in a torrential downpour.

And all Julia could do was stand there, looking out, thinking, *When it rains, it pours.*

Chapter Three

No one learns gin rummy in a vacuum; you need an opponent because the game is more than rules.

Four massive windows lined the front of the bookstore, looking out onto Utica Square. It had long been one of Julia's favorite pieces of real estate, but as she gazed at the windows, she was oblivious to the women who pushed strollers behind her and the people who were settling down for lunch at the outdoor cafés. She didn't feel the clean, cool breeze that blew her hair away from her face, washing away any memory of August's heat and February's cold—making any normal woman think that it was the perfect Indian summer day. But not Julia. She couldn't move, couldn't speak, couldn't do anything but stare into the four massive windows, each one overflowing with copies of *Ninety-Day Engagement* and Sadie Whitaker's smiling, Botoxed face.

Julia looked at the *Ninety-Day Engagement* cover with

its glossy finish and gold foil letters. Its message was simple: Women were ninety days away from lounging on fainting couches while wearing black Donna Karen dresses and diamond chokers from Harry Winston; they were ninety days away from Mr. Right and perfectly quaffed hair. Julia stood staring at four full windows of red velvet and twinkle lights, crystal chandeliers and champagne flutes, each sending out a message, calling to the masses, telling the women of the world that they, too, could be ninety days away from perfection.

Julia had told women they could be okay on their own. She'd tried to help them improve themselves and find peace and happiness and a richer sense of self. Sadie helped them land a husband. Sadie had all four windows.

Beside her, Nina said, "This is a disgrace!" and Julia felt an odd sense of relief, knowing that she couldn't be upset about another author getting more window space than Julia had ever received—she had to be too professional, too confident, too poised for such pettiness.

"This is just outrageous," Nina said. "I'm talking to a manager."

"No, Nina," Julia said. "Don't do that." *Please do that.*

"Someone's got to save these people from themselves," Nina shot back, and Julia thought, *I have the best friend ever!*

"Do you see the way that fake chandelier throws off the

symmetry of the whole display?" Nina stopped and gestured to the nearby window. "And those *pedestals*! I'm going to have to get to the bottom of this."

Julia stayed on the sidewalk and watched her best friend appear in the window moments later, a salesgirl in tow. Nina gestured wildly, and the girl tried to stop her from moving stacks of books or ripping down the white twinkle lights that framed the top of the display. Then, the girl gave up, and so did Julia.

As soon as she walked inside, Julia forgot all about the windows and about Lance and his new West Coast digs. She breathed in the aroma of all those books and felt like the mother ship was calling her home.

"Miss James?" Julia spun to see an assistant manager coming toward her. "It's Mindy," she said. "I helped with your last signing."

"Of course, Mindy. Hi," Julia said. "And please, call me Julia." *Because I'm not mad about the windows, and I'm very approachable and down-to-earth, and I'm not really that old, am I?*

"Wow," Mindy said, beaming. "It's really good to see you. I was hoping you'd be in soon."

"You were?" Julia said, amazed by the shock in her voice. She glanced toward the tables where her three books were usually displayed. "Do you need me to sign some . . ." But her voice trailed off as she saw that her books were nowhere to be found, and instead, her usual tables were covered with even more copies of Sadie Whitaker's face with just a little Dr. Phil thrown in.

"Oh no," Mindy said. "I think we've got lots of autographed copies of your books left. In fact, I think we had to move some of them to the storeroom—we can't send them back to the publisher and get our money back after they've been signed, you know," Mindy added.

Behind Mindy, Nina was shouting, "And can someone please find me an extension cord!" So Julia leaned forward, gave Mindy all of her attention.

"See," the girl was saying, "I read this book, and it was talking about the importance of networking, and I asked myself, I said, *Self, who do you know who could help you?* I came up with a pretty big list, you know? Like there's this guy, and he owns this business, and he comes in here all the time looking for the new John Grisham even though I've told him it isn't out yet, and that I'll call him when we get it in, but he still comes by. So I know him," Mindy said, holding out a finger as she caught her breath. "And I know this lady who works at—"

"And you know me," Julia said brightly, hoping that's where the story was eventually heading.

"Exactly!" Mindy cried. "I know Julia James! And that's really freakin' cool." She stopped suddenly and brought her hand to her lips. "Oops, pardon my language."

"That's really freakin' okay," Julia told her. Mindy blushed.

"So, yeah, I know you. And I told myself, *Self, maybe Ms. James—*"

"Julia," Julia corrected again.

"Yeah, but at the time I was calling you Ms. James," Mindy explained.

"Of course." Julia gestured for the girl to carry on.

Mindy inched closer to Julia and lowered her voice. "See, the reason I was hoping to talk to you was because I've been doing some writing myself and—"

"Oh, Mindy," Julia jumped to cut her off. "I haven't mentored anyone in—"

"No," the young woman hurried to say. "I'm not looking for writing advice from you."

Julia felt herself jerk back. She knew this conversation. She'd *had* this conversation, and this definitely wasn't a part of the script. "You're not?"

"No. I was just wondering if you'd give Lance my screenplay."

Somehow Julia found a way to separate herself from Mindy. Did she say yes? Did she say no? She wasn't really sure.

By that time Nina might have been ripping down wallpaper or mixing up paint, but Julia was lost in the tall shelves, thinking, remembering what her plan had been at the beginning of the summer: Give up solitaire, remodel the house, learn to play gin in both the literal and figurative senses of the word. Somehow she knew that meant leaving Julia James, champion of the single woman, behind her. But the question remained, Who was she supposed to be now?

She felt Nina come up behind her. "Oh, here you are," Nina said, sounding slightly out of breath. "What are you doing?"

Julia thought, *That's the million-dollar question.* Seriously. She would have paid a million bucks to know what she was supposed to do next.

They walked together through the aisles filled with thousands and thousands of volumes—an ocean of words—and Julia knew, really knew, that without the security of a best-selling name, how easy it would be to drown there.

"Hey, Neen, what would you do if you never had to worry about money and you could do anything in the world you wanted to do?"

Nina skipped ahead. She picked up an art book and flipped through the pages. "I am doing what I want to do."

"Oh," Julia said, suddenly jealous of her best friend, but that feeling disappeared as soon as Julia heard the words, "Well, hello, Tiny."

Chapter Four

Of all the skills necessary for gin, a good memory is the most essential, because the only way to win is to remember what has been discarded and why.

Hello, Jason," Julia said. Nina said nothing. They'd all known each other since elementary school, and yet they stood there like strangers. But standing in her ex-husband's shadow Nina seemed to be growing smaller if that was even possible, and Julia had to wonder how love can turn so hot and cold. She hoped she never found out.

Jason had grown a goatee, or something like it, just a random puff of hair that grazed his lower lip, and she could make out the glittering gold of a new pinkie ring. He looked like a new kind of superhero, Julia thought: Midlife-Crisis Man.

Then he leaned toward her, and said, "How's the *boy-*

friend, Jules?" Julia was pretty sure that was supposed to be an insult, a very clever, very witty remark intended to burn.

"You're too sweet, Jason," Julia said as sweetly as possible. "Actually, Lance is doing very well. They have him training for this big action movie right now. He's working with one of the premiere martial arts experts in the world." She remembered how Jason had tried—and failed—to bully Lance like he bullied everyone else, so she smiled her brightest smile and said, "And he *always* asks about you."

Jason's jaw clenched and he swallowed hard, and Julia thought, *Well, my work here is done.*

But then she looked at Nina—a person who had always been petite and slim and almost childlike in so many ways it was easy to forget she was a woman; but there was no little girl left in her then. And worse, there was no fight. Julia would have given anything to have her lash out—cuss, yell, throw things—anything but stand there like a broken piece of porcelain, a doll that's lost her shine.

"Come on, Neen," Julia said with a tug, but Nina's gaze and body were frozen. She wasn't looking at Jason. No, her eyes were glued to the girl walking toward them—the one Julia had last seen in a black-and-white newspaper wedding announcement that Nina had ceremoniously burned on Julia's stove.

"Jay," the girl called. "They won't have the new *Modern*

Bride in until next week," she said, pouting as she draped herself over Jason's arm.

"Jay?" Julia asked.

"It's what the guys call me—in the company ball league. Big Jay," he said with a wink.

"Hello, I'm Julia," Julia said as she extended a hand toward the young woman. "You can call me Little Jay."

No one laughed, which Julia thought was just as well. Nothing was funny.

"Oh," Jason said, draping his arm around his fiancée. "This is Madison. Madison, this is Julia and Nina. My ex." He said it in a way that made Nina sound like an exhibit in the Jason Rhinehart Museum, something subtitled *Wife Number One: The Early Years.*

"Hi," Madison said. Nina, however, said nothing.

Julia knew that Nina was either dying or ticking away like a very silent, very lethal bomb, so she grasped her friend's arm, tried to pull her away, but before they could budge, Jason's hand reached out, holding Nina, keeping her from moving forward.

"I was going to put this in the mail, but since you're here . . ."

Then he handed her a check—one of *The Checks.* Julia looked at it, and then at him. A small smile stained his lips as he looked down at the slim piece of paper, daring her to take it. It was a small smile, a small gesture, even a small check in the grand scheme of things, but Julia knew it was a part of something larger. A monthly installment of something worth much, much more. So in that second Julia understood why Jason didn't fight the alimony portion of their divorce, that it was a small price to pay to keep Nina on her string.

Rip it up, Julia silently chanted, willing her best friend to throw it in his face, shove it down his throat—do one of a thousand very "Nina" things that she seemed incapable of doing when Jason was around. Julia would have traded Nina a million dollars for the satisfaction of seeing her say no, but Nina could only look at the man she'd loved since second grade, then at her replacement.

Then she silently put *The Check* in her purse and walked away.

Chapter Five

If a player calls gin by mistake and lays down his cards, he may finish out the hand, but he will play under the handicap of having already laid his cards on the table.

The phone is ringing, Julia realized but didn't reach for it. The sound pierced the air but not her veil of sleep. She rolled over and tried to shake the ringing from her mind, then suddenly thought, *Oh crap, the phone's ringing!*

She scrambled from the bed, but her legs were tangled in the sheet and she fell. Her knee hit the hardwood floor with a sharp crack that left her crying out in pain, but the phone rang on like a high-tech game of Marco Polo in the dark.

"Did I *wake* you?" His voice was so clear and strong that Julia thought for a moment about closing her eyes and imagining that he was just down the hall instead of thousands of miles away. She rubbed her aching knee. She leaned her back against the foot of the bed and listened as Lance said, "Were you actually sleeping?" He sounded amazed, impressed, like someone who really knew her, and Julia kept her eyes wide open.

"Yes," she said through a schoolgirl grin. "I've been sleeping great." *An insomniac's favorite sentence.*

"Do you want me to—"

"Don't even think about hanging up that phone," Julia snapped.

She crawled onto the bed and, under the heavy blankets, found a warm place in the chilly room.

Through the line she heard music and laughing and had to ask, "Where are you?"

"Oh," he said, yelling over the noise. "Some party. I don't know. They just threw me in a suit and told me I had to stay for twenty minutes." There was static and muffled voices on the line then Lance was back, saying, "George says hi."

"George?" Julia asked.

"Clooney."

Oh my gosh! "You told George Clooney about me?"

"It's his phone I'm borrowing."

I can star-sixty-nine George Clooney!

"He's so sexy!" Julia exclaimed without really remembering who she was speaking to.

"Yeah," Lance said. "That's the rumor."

"What did you say about me?"

"I said you were mean and ugly and under no circumstances was he ever to flirt with you."

"Okay," Julia said, laughing, remembering. "You're kind of sexy, too."

"Yeah." She heard him smile. "That's another rumor."

A long silence filled the line as she looked around the darkened room. "You were great this morning."

"Really?"

"Oh, yeah. You handled everything really well—the stuff about how you were tending bar a year ago and then everything with your dad and . . ."

"And what?"

"And when she sprung that on you about the house."

Suddenly the embroidery on Julia's sheets became very interesting to her. He wasn't there, but she still couldn't risk him looking her in the eye.

"Sugar," he said, but for some reason Julia laughed.

"Sugar?"

"Yeah." He sounded only slightly offended. "What's wrong with sugar?"

"Nothing if you're putting it in tea."

"Well, I'll keep trying on the pet name front. How's that sound?"

"Sounds good."

In the background, the party raged on, but outside Julia's

window, tree frogs serenaded the last warm night. She didn't know where he was, but she knew he had to be a million miles away.

"I didn't know you were thinking about doing that. Congratulations," she tried, but the words came out hollow, empty.

"Wes found a place. He said it was a good investment. It's a great deal. I haven't even seen the house, but it made sense, so I bought it."

"You just bought it?" she asked, not understanding. "Sight unseen?"

"Well, yeah. I trust Wes with this stuff. That's why I hired him. You have no idea how . . ." But then he trailed off. "I just need someplace to stay when I'm out there."

"When are you going to be in California?"

"Julia, I'm an actor. I will have to spend time in California. Like for the *Wisdom of Solomon* premiere. This is a big deal, Julia. These people take this stuff seriously."

Of course they do, she thought but didn't say. Of course he should buy a house—it was his money. His life.

"Julia, I'm sorry I didn't tell you."

Of course he was sorry, because Lance was perfect and the perfect people always know what to say.

"Julia, I want you to come. I've been asking you to come for weeks."

"Lance," Julia found the strength to say finally. "It's just really not a good time—with the roof situation and Jason getting remarried and—"

"Stop. Hold it right there." Miraculously, she did as she was told. "First of all, last I checked, you weren't a roofer. And you're not a wedding planner, so I think Jason can get remarried without you."

The silence stretched out between them for a long time as Julia remembered that's what she missed most about him— the silences. It had taken thirty-four years for her to find someone to be quiet with, and now when he spoke, it was a single word: *"Come."*

What would *I* do in California? Julia wanted to say. Then she seriously wondered, what *would* I do in California? She didn't have friends or family there. No job. Nothing that, by her usual standards, constituted a life. But she had Lance. Julia had heard of girls who would pack up and rearrange their lives over a boyfriend. Always before, Julia had thought they were pathetic, but now she wondered if they might actually be brave. Julia didn't know. She just knew she wasn't one of them.

"I bet it's really nice," she said. "It sounds nice."

"Yeah," Lance said. "It is, I think, but Julia, it really is just real estate. A permanent address and all."

Permanent addresses—Julia hadn't given them much thought since she left college. Even now, she still got credit card applications and frequent flyer statements at her parents' home. Lance hadn't had that, she told herself. How many schools had he attended? Ten, twelve, something like that. It was his money. It was his life. It was permanent.

In California.

"Hey," he said, "I've got to go."

"Yeah," she said, smiling weakly. "Thanks for calling. I know how busy you are and—"

"I'll talk to you later."

"Yeah." She nodded. "Good luck with everything."

"Julia?" he said, and she silently prayed, *Ask me again.* "Good night."

Julia lay down on the bed, still clutching the cordless phone, but she didn't want to call George Clooney. There was particleboard overhead, keeping the weather out until the new roof could go on, but Julia wished it wasn't there. She wanted to see the stars—the real ones—the kind a girl can wish on.

She knew she was supposed to close her eyes and go back to sleep, but she also knew it wouldn't happen. Even without solitaire to pass the time, Julia knew she'd be awake for hours, so she just lay there, thinking about a sky she couldn't see.

"You've got to go, Jules."

The voice made her jump upright and her heart pound. She looked to the doorway and saw Nina.

"You're gonna go," her best friend said. "And you're gonna take me with you."

Chapter Six

You will learn to classify the cards as absolutely safe, fairly safe, somewhat unsafe, and completely wild. It's important to decide early on which ones you want to carry with you.

Julia looked around the airport terminal and tried to figure out what felt so wrong—why she'd spent her moments at the counter wishing that her credit card would be denied (it wasn't); or that they wouldn't have any first-class seats available (they did); or that some well-meaning airline employee would get on the staticky PA system and announce that all flights from Tulsa to LAX were going to be grounded. Indefinitely. (They weren't.)

She'd flown a hundred times. She'd seen half the world. And yet, for some reason she kept staring through the long glass windows at the gleaming silver jet, feeling like she was about to take a maiden voyage.

Feeling, in a word, like Nina.

"It's a good plane, isn't it?" Nina asked again, oblivious to the long line of people behind her. She ignored the shifting, murmuring crowd as she stood higher on her tiptoes, leaned farther onto the counter, and gripped her ticket. "I mean, you'd fly on it, wouldn't you?" she asked, her normally deep voice striking an unfamiliar high note. "*Have* you flown on that plane?"

The woman behind the counter smiled a broad, toothy smile that made Julia wonder if she'd rubbed Vaseline on her teeth like they do at the Miss America Pageant. Then, she glanced at Julia—a *help me out here* glance—but Julia shrugged, so the woman turned back to Nina and smiled another big Vaseliney smile. "I've flown on DC-10s many times."

"But what about *that* plane?" Nina demanded. "And what about the pilot? Is he any good? Because let me tell you, I've been driving since I was twelve and—"

"Ma'am, our pilots are fully qualified."

"But a highway patrolman once told me that I had the most natural gift for acceleration he had ever seen," Nina blurted. "He said, *The way you fly, you ought to be a pilot.* Right, Julia?"

"Yeah," Julia said, although she'd been too nauseous at the time to remember much more of that particular conversation.

"Have a nice flight, ladies," the attendant said in her *move along now* voice, but Nina didn't move along. She was frozen. Petrified. Completely incapable of budging from that spot.

"Can anyone sit in the copilot's chair," Nina asked, "or does that require some sort of certificate or—"

"Nina!" Julia snapped, this time not caring how it sounded. Julia knew it was the thought of going so fast and so far in something she wasn't driving that made Nina stand there, practically bolted to the terminal floor.

The sun glistened off the sleek, silver body of the plane outside as Nina turned to Julia and whispered, "Come on, Jules, let's just drive, okay? You. Me. The open road. We can get our kicks on Route Sixty-Six. It'll be—"

"Nina," Julia said calmly, cutting her off. "The premiere is the day after tomorrow. We'll practically have to drive nonstop—"

"I can do it."

"We already have our tickets."

"It's only money. You have lots of money."

Yes, Julia remembered, she did have lots of money, but Nina didn't. Nina had *The Checks* and Jason and . . .

Julia saw the color draining from Nina's cherub-like face, and Julia felt herself sway. The daze she'd been in since Lance's call was starting to break, so she had to get on that plane—right then. They couldn't wait a day or an hour more, and most of all, she couldn't drive to California because the road there was long and hard, with an exit sign every mile or so—fifteen hundred chances to turn the car around.

"Ma'am," the ticket agent said, "see here." She took her thumb and forefinger and pinched the ticket in Nina's hand. "You are in 3C. It's on the aisle. It's a very good seat—a first-class seat."

"Yeah, Neen, not many people get to take their first flight in first class," Julia added quickly.

"And first class has big comfy seats," the attendant said.

"And warm nuts," Julia remembered.

"And fresh-baked chocolate chip cookies . . ." the attendant said wistfully.

"And free booze," said a man behind them.

"Planes are fun!" Nina said forty minutes later as she held the tiny bottle of vodka against the light of the flight attendant call button and watched the last drop of silvery liquid slosh inside. She seemed to revel in the dollhouse proportions of the little bottle, the little buttons on the ceiling. The little carts. The little plastic forks for eating little TV dinners with little servings of chicken cordon bleu. Every frequent flier Julia had ever known complained about the narrow seats and cramped surroundings, but Nina acted as if she'd been waiting her entire life to find a place built exactly to her scale.

Of course, the vodka didn't hurt.

"Aren't planes fun?" Nina asked the man across the aisle who was glued to his *Wall Street Journal*. She patted his arm, reveling in the texture of his Brooks Brothers suit while he pretended she didn't exist, even when she leaned closer and whispered, "I *love* flying."

Julia reached across the seat and grabbed her best friend by her shoulders and pulled her back across the aisle. "Yeah, Neen," Julia said, as she glanced around at the cabin full of staring people. "Did you know your seat reclines? Did you know you can take a nap?"

Julia tried to pry the bottle from her hand, but Nina pushed her aside and yelled, "Jason's an idiot!" Then she looked at her best friend. Her face was part obstinate child, part woman-on-a-mission. "He told me I couldn't go to that business conference in Cancun because I hate to fly. But I *loooove* flying!" she cried as she climbed onto her knees and looked all around the first-class cabin.

"Jason's an idiot!" she said again like it was brand-new information. She looked down at Julia with a terrifying sort of purpose that, in Julia's experience, was usually followed by trips to the emergency room and/or bail money. She nodded in defiance as she said, "I should tell him he's an idiot."

Julia sat perfectly still in her leather chair and no longer cursed her small friend's carrying voice or inability to be knocked unconscious. *I should tell him he's an idiot.* The sentence echoed through the cabin, and instead of wishing the words would go away, Julia hoped that everyone, from the pilot to the poor soul in 47C, would hear them. She had been waiting her whole life to hear Nina say something of the sort. *Maybe I should have gotten her drunk and put her on a plane years ago,* Julia thought, realizing the power in vodka and thirty thousand feet of perspective.

"Yes," Julia said finally, "you *should* tell him that."

"Good! Right!" Nina chirped. "Will do!"

Nina leaned back in her seat, and Julia finally felt safe in closing her eyes. She felt her head fall to the window, and waited for fatigue to wipe her mind blank and sleep to take her, then she heard someone yell, "Cell phone!"

Julia bolted upright and ripped the device from Nina's hand before she could punch SEND.

"Tell you what, Neen. Why don't we call Jason *after* we land?"

"But—"

"Or you could write him a letter," Julia offered. "A nice, old-fashioned letter that he can save and read over and over again."

The idea of eternal torment must have appealed to Nina because she ripped a piece of paper from the legal pad on the tray in front of Mr. 3A and asked Julia for a pen.

Dear Jason,

I am on plane. Far far above ground and everything looks tiny—especially you!!!

I am going to California with Julia, but while I'm there I'll probably become very, very famous because you won't be there to embarrass me by sending back your meat one hundred million bazillion times and snapping at the waiter and, oh yeah, WHAT THE HELL IS THAT THING ON YOUR LIP? Gross. On behalf of women everywhere, gross! Gross! Gross! Gross! Gross!

(FYI women aren't impressed by men who spend that much time thinking about their own faces. It shows they don't have anything better to do . . . like build stuff or cure a disease or something.) And while you're at it, lose the pinkie ring, Elton.

I am just so very happy to be NOT MARRIED TO YOU because many, many NICE men want to marry me. In fact, very nice business traveler-type man in 3A has just said he will marry me if his wife has tragic accident or terrible Lifetime Television for Women-type disease. Just wrote my phone number on his hand with lucky blue ink pen to seal the deal!!!

So see, I'm going to be wonderful, tanned, Mrs. 3A living in California. You are more than welcome to come visit. You can stay in the pool house (like on The O.C.).

Okay, just asked Mr. 3A if he has pool house, and he

said no but that if he married me we could move, so see,
there's a place to for you stay . . . in my pool house!!!

So, I'll send you a postcard when I get there or an in-
vitation to my wedding to Mr. 3A or at least a card with
the address of our pool house!

~~Love,~~ ~~Sincerely,~~ ~~Best~~ ~~Wishes,~~ *Good-bye forever!*
Nina

Julia read the note over and over then folded it carefully
and placed it in her purse. When she looked up, she saw the
flight attendant leaning toward her.

"I think she's out now," Julia whispered, pointing toward a snoring Nina.

"Oh, that's great," the attendant said. "I just . . . you
know . . . I overheard her. And I wanted to tell you about
this book. It's by this woman, Sadie Whitaker . . ."

Chapter Seven

As Julia sat in the convertible, going nowhere, she thought her senses were in overdrive—like someone had hit PAUSE and so she had longer than usual to smell, taste, and feel. Exhaust from the cement truck in front of them wafted into the car. The sounds of honking and creeping traffic took her back to her first studio apartment in New York, where the city that never sleeps worked the graveyard shift outside her bedroom window—buses and taxis and ambulances running through the night. The sun fell upon her face and arms with so much heat that she would have sworn it was July—not October—and that her mother's voice would soon come cutting through the air, warning her that redheads always burn.

"Exit three miles ahead." Julia jumped when she heard the warning, knowing the voice definitely didn't belong to her mother. "Prepare to exit three miles ahead."

"Ugh!" Nina cried beside her. "We know already!" Then her best friend started banging on the console at the navigational system that had seemed like such a good idea at the time—before they realized it was programmed to warn them whenever they approached an exit—even if they were moving at a whopping two miles an hour, crawling along the interstate like ants across the blistering asphalt.

"Exit three miles ahead."

"Let me drive," Nina said, but her heart wasn't in it—if it was, her leg would have been over the center console and not even the California Highway Patrol would have been enough to stop her from carjacking her best friend then and there.

Julia raised her hand to shield her eyes. The brightness bore down around them through a day that didn't feel like fall and didn't feel like summer. Everything was too loud, too crass, and Julia couldn't shake the feeling that she and Nina were both about to sober up.

"Exit two point eight miles ahead," the electronic voice chimed, but Julia could only look at the convertibles, SUVs, and eighteen-wheelers that sat packed around them, going nowhere.

"Lance hasn't hired a decorator yet, has he?" Nina

asked. "Because if he has, you're gonna have to fire her and hire me."

"*I'm* going to have to fire her?" Julia said.

"Sure. You're the lady of the house. You have the final say in things like decorators."

"Nina, I'm not the 'lady of the house,'" Julia said, not wanting to put any labels on anything—especially not that one. It sounded suspiciously illegal.

But Nina only rolled her eyes and said, "Sure you are. I've read Jane Austen." Then something seemed to occur to her. "Lance doesn't have an old maid sister, does he?"

"He has a mother."

"Oh." Nina sank into the seat and pulled her knees up against her chest, wrapping them with her arms. "He'd better not have hired a decorator."

When the traffic finally parted and the electronic voice finally told them to turn, Julia eased the convertible onto Mulholland Drive. A cool breeze wafted in the shadow that splashed across the road as it curved higher and higher into the hills, and Nina's Hermès scarf billowed in the breeze. Julia prayed it was a knockoff.

"Nice scarf," she said.

Nina jerked the rearview mirror in her direction to examine the effect. "It's new."

"It's expensive," Julia added, but Nina didn't say anything.

In that rearview mirror, Nina saw only bright colors and pretty shapes. Julia saw *The Checks* and Jason.

When the computer told them to make one more turn, Nina let out a low whistle and said, "Speaking of expensive."

♥

"Do I just drive in?" Julia asked, not knowing if it was her right to turn onto the forty-foot drive, toward the towering mass of cream-colored walls and wrought-iron railings—sun decks, and balconies, and ocean views that looked, frankly, like every other French provincial mansion they'd seen since leaving the freeway. Still, Julia knew to keep her emphasis on *mansion*.

The wrought-iron gate stood open, like an invitation. Or a dare.

She glanced down at the computer in the dash. "Surely this isn't the right place." She started pushing buttons. "I mean . . ." She glanced back at the home, the gates, the sweeping, manicured grounds. "Surely this isn't . . ."

But then the digitized voice said again, "You have reached your final destination," and Julia had no choice but to believe it. She parked the car in the circle drive, got out, and walked to where Nina was already standing on the brick driveway, staring up at the towering walls.

"Kinda makes up for not having a Malibu Barbie Dream

House, huh?" Nina asked, but the only thing Barbie-related Julia could remember was how she hadn't had a Ken doll, so her Barbie went to the pretend Barbie prom alone. Then Julia went to the real prom alone.

It was one of many things she held in reserve for the day when she broke down and started seeing a shrink, so she just shrugged and said, "If Barbie were real, she wouldn't have room in her waist for kidneys. She'd have to carry them in her purse."

"Sure." Nina looked at her. "But she'd have a kick-ass house."

Leave it to Nina to keep everything in perspective.

As they stood together in the shade of the house, Julia peeked through the glass in the door and saw marble floors and curving staircases, but not a trace of another living, breathing creature. A sense of relief passed over her, as if she'd almost been caught spying on another family—another life. At someplace she didn't belong. She remembered her own house—the one without a roof.

"Neen, maybe we should—"

But Nina had already rung the doorbell, and chimes were reverberating through the house. It was a classical melody, but Julia couldn't name the composer or the key. She felt herself sink a little lower, wondering whether or not she belonged in a house where even the doorbell was more cultured than she was.

She didn't know she'd turned and started back toward the car until she felt Nina grab her arm.

"Wait a sec. It might take an hour or two for someone to get to the door in this place."

So Julia stayed there, staring straight up at the towering structure. "It's so big. Why would Lance buy something so . . . Can you imagine how much it will cost to heat it? Or cool it? Or—"

"*Decorate it*," Nina said, almost salivating.

Nina rang the bell again.

The silence that followed must have stretched on for longer than even Julia realized, because eventually Nina turned to her and asked, "Someone was supposed to be here, right?"

"Well . . ." Julia tried, but before she could say another word, the massive doors swung open.

The woman in the doorway wasn't tiny like Nina was tiny. Nina was petite, almost childlike. The girl in the doorway was actually about Julia's height, but she couldn't have weighed more than a hundred and ten pounds. She had long, noodle-like arms that seemed to be the result of being stretched too much as a child. And yet she didn't look sick, like she'd been battling some terrible disease. Health and vigor radiated off her. Her shoulder-length blond hair gleamed. She was the reason men have been inspired to sing about California girls.

Julia really, really tried not to hate her.

Then, the girl threw her arms around Nina and cried, "Julia!" They hugged. They swayed. They were forged together in an instant bond of best friends foreverness. Then the girl pulled away and said, "I'm just so glad to finally meet *the* Julia James!"

"Oh, um—" Nina started but the girl was dragging her through the door.

"I am such a huge fan," the girl squealed. "When I heard you were coming, I was like, that's so cool, gotta get the house opened up for her. You know?"

Julia followed them inside, but as soon as her foot touched the smooth, cool marble, she forgot what she was going to say. Instead, Julia wanted to yell—not to correct the girl, but just to see if it would echo. She was betting it would.

The girl closed the door behind them, slid a chain, and pulled a drapery panel farther across the window, blocking out the view, casting the space in shadow. Now, instead of yelling, Julia thought they should whisper.

"I'm just so glad you're here!" The girl hugged Nina again, but instead of correcting her, Julia started to wonder what it would be like to go through the rest of her life with Nina as her proxy, her double. Nina could do her interviews. Nina could read her reviews. Nina could take her chances like the natural-born stuntwoman she was. Julia looked around and saw empty walls—a blank slate. She wondered who she might become in California.

"I was totally thinking about you this morning," the girl said, talking as fast as Nina liked to drive, but Julia wasn't really listening. For once in Julia's life, words didn't matter. "And I was wondering if you were going to like the house and stuff, and that made me think about this one time when I was at this party at Bruce Willis's house and"—she drew a haggard breath—"long-story-short . . . avocados!" The girl laughed, and then Nina gave Julia a *are you going to correct her or should I* look, but Julia was too busy making up another name and deciding what kind of accent she could speak in—this new Julia. California Julia. She was going to start calling people "darling" and giving double-cheek kisses without the sarcasm. She was going to know what song the dad-gum doorbell was playing.

"Lance is going to be so happy to see you!" the girl squealed.

But then Nina took the girl's arms that were reaching out to her and pushed them toward Julia, passing the *hugger* off to the rightful *huggee.*

"*That's* Julia—the girlfriend. I'm Nina—the decorator."

And just like that, Julia's charade was over. It hadn't even really begun. She never got to try the double-cheek kiss maneuver. It was just as well. She knew she'd never pull it off.

"Hi," Julia said finally with a guilty, sorry-I-let-you-make-a-fool-of-yourself-for-so-long wave.

But if the girl felt like a fool, she hid it well. "Hi! I'm Amanda, Lance's personal assistant," she said as she pulled Julia into a tight hug. "Like I said, I'm a huge fan!"

Chapter Eight

By knowing what you need, gin becomes a game more of skill than chance.

Julia spent her first night in a Hollywood mansion sleeping side by side with Nina in the queen bed that Lance had shipped from his studio apartment in New York. The headboard was made of particleboard. The mattress was lumpy, and the pillows were as hard as stone, but as Julia looked at the thrift store furniture—the mismatched dresser with its cracked mirror—she knew somehow that Lance had already used up his seven years of bad luck.

It says a lot about a person, Julia thought, not what they keep so much as what they can't throw away. She saw the things that Lance had chosen to carry with him. It made her love him more.

Nina, however, appeared in the bedroom door with her

freshly washed face, her freshly brushed teeth, and announced, "Of course, this has all got to go." She knocked on the frail headboard with her knuckles as if to prove a point, but all Julia could do was remember how Amanda had bounced from empty room to empty room, flicking soft lights off and on, momentarily illuminating one pale space after another, until they'd found that room. That furniture.

Julia pulled the covers to her chin and confessed, "I kinda like it."

Nina scooted down into the bed and said, "You kinda would."

She turned onto her side, away from Nina, and she hoped that a man who didn't mind a lumpy pillow wouldn't mind a woman with lumpy thighs. She wrapped her arms around the house's piece of imperfection, closed her eyes, and tried to sleep.

They lay side by side for a long time before Nina's soft voice said, "Sometimes I wish he'd hit me."

Julia bolted upright, turned, and looked at Nina. There was no asking who *he* was—no doubt at all. Even though the house was dark, there was still light in the room—ambient light. City light. The kind country people never get used to. She saw the outline of Nina's face—a face she knew even better than her own. She expected to see tears, if not on her cheeks then welling in her eyes, but Nina was calm, resolute.

"If he'd hit me, I would have left sooner," Nina finished,

and Julia wondered if it was true. Nina was all action, no talk. She had perfected the art of redecorating Jason's words, his meaning. A hit would have been different, though. Nina wasn't one to cover bruises like she brightened rooms with fresh coats of paint.

"Yeah," Julia said slowly, letting the truth sink in. "You would have left. But first you would have hit him back," she said, amazed when she realized how true it was, wondering how it had never occurred to her until then.

"Yeah." Nina pulled the covers up to her chin, smiling at the memory of a punch she'd never landed.

"And then your dad and my dad and half of Mayes County would have finished the job," Julia added.

Nina's smiled widened. She looked safe, like someone on the brink of being happy. "And Lance," she said then, as if he shouldn't be forgotten.

Julia eased back down on the pillow. She sank into a warm spot on the bed. "And Lance."

◆

Lance saw the sun come up. Standing in front of the hotel windows, he looked out onto Central Park, saw the Technicolor light sweep across the trees that held on to the very last of summer's leaves. He sipped a cup of coffee and looked toward the phone, and his fingers involuntarily punched the numbers against the porcelain mug.

"Now, *People* is going to be here in forty minutes," the kid said behind him. "And Marc is on the line with *ET* right now, and . . ." The young man went on, but Lance didn't hear a word. He just watched the sun, the day, come into his hotel room, one second at a time.

"Is there anything we can get you before we—"

"Yeah," Lance said, turning. "I just need a second." He moved toward the phone, but the young man didn't budge. "To make a call," Lance added. "You know . . . Kind of a personal kind of thing."

"Oh, right," the young man said, punching the air with his frail fist. "I'll just . . ." He motioned to the tray on the table with Lance's half-eaten breakfast. "Is there anything else you need? Bagel? Newspaper? Diuretic?"

"Uh . . . no," Lance muttered. "No, I think I'm good." He stepped toward the bedside phone, but the young man was instantly in his way.

"I can get housekeeping to come make up that bed. Here, let me call . . ."

"No," Lance said. "The bed is fine."

"How about some more coffee or juice or—"

"Juice," Lance said. "Sure. I'd love some—"

"Apple? Grape? Crangrape? Orange?"

"Orange," Lance snapped.

The young man took a step toward the door, but spun suddenly and asked, "Low pulp? No pulp? Heavy—?"

"Pulp free!" Lance said as he took the young man by the arm and steered him toward the bedroom door.

He sank down on the bed, breathed deeply, and picked up the receiver. Moments later, he heard her pick up on the second ring.

"Hey," he said softly with a glance at the clock. It was late there—or early—but somehow he knew it wouldn't really matter. Not to her. "You are a very hard woman to get ahold of."

"Who would ever need to talk to me?" she asked, but not in that tone of normal mothers—the guilty, *tell me how much you need me* tone. Lance knew that Donna Collins didn't have hidden agendas. He knew that, for a woman who'd spent her entire life working in theater, she almost never acted.

For a moment the hotel suite was silent, and he sat perfectly still, waiting. His mother's breathing came through the line. She sounded close, but then, in the other room, phones rang. People scurried and yelled.

"Sometimes *I* need to talk to you," he said, meaning it. "I'll get you a—"

"I don't want a cell phone," she said. "I have no idea how or why a device without wires has people more tied down than ever before, but it does."

In the other room he heard, "Will someone get me a strainer?" He laughed.

"What's so funny?" his mother asked.

"Pulp," he said. The long silence that stretched out told him that he'd stumped her.

"You hate pulp," she said, sounding confused.

"Yeah," he said, "that's okay. I don't think I'm going to have to worry about it ever again." *I have people for my pulp,* he thought but couldn't say. Somehow, he knew she wouldn't think it was funny.

He played with the phone cord, stretching it out and back again—a childlike impulse brought to the surface by the sound of his mother's voice.

"Hey," he said quickly, needing to move before he lost his nerve. "I'm calling about tomorrow night. I was wondering if you were—"

"Did you invite your father?"

He should have seen the question coming, but he hadn't.

"I invited *you*," he said.

"It's not a mutually exclusive proposition, dear," she said.

Yeah, but it's supposed to be, he thought. Suddenly, right then, he felt cheated because his parents' divorce hadn't come with people hurling insults and trying to buy his love. Suddenly, civility seemed a cruel and unusual fate. Passionate love should become passionate hate. There was nothing worse than watching it fade to nothing, the ashes of a fire that has burned itself out.

On the phone, his mother was saying, "Lance, I'm proud of you. So proud. But I don't think I'll be coming. I'm terribly busy with rehearsals here, and you know how I hate to drive, and . . . Well, to be honest, darling, it's really not my scene."

Of course not, Lance wanted to say, but couldn't. In the next room, a half-dozen strangers were pouring orange juice through coffee filters. It was as far away from Donna Collins's scene as he could be, but he didn't say so. He just waited, watching the sun spread across the buildings outside.

"I think you should ask your father," his mother said, but Lance shook his head as if she could see him, as if she would listen. "He would want to be there. He'd understand. He'd—"

"Mom, you won't have to worry about a thing, okay? I can have my stylist bring some clothes and—"

"I have clothes, Lance," she nearly snapped, reminding him that his mother was a woman for whom clothes were just clothes—not a statement, or a PR stunt. She was just a woman who didn't want to be naked.

"I know. I'm sorry," he blurted, wondering why everything was coming out wrong. "I just want to see you, that's all. It's my first movie—my first premiere. I want you to be there."

"I saw your premiere—you were Pinocchio that year we

lived in Oregon." She laughed. It was a beautiful sound. "Remember that? Half the cast came down with food poisoning, but you'd been to every practice and knew all the lines. That was your debut, dear. And you were marvelous."

How could he argue with that?

"Well, you're going to have to come down soon, okay? I want to see you, and for you to see my new house and . . ." He trailed off, suddenly remembering the obvious. "I want you to meet Julia. She's there. She decided to come out for the premiere."

"Oh, did she?"

Lance couldn't help but smile. "She's already there—at the house—with her friend, Nina. I told you about her, didn't I? The interior decorator."

"Oh," his mother said. "So Julia's decorating?"

"No, it's not . . . well, knowing Nina, they probably are doing something, but—"

"That's nice, dear. I've got to go, though, darling."

"Yeah," Lance said. "Sure, and if you change your mind about the premiere . . . You know you're invited, right?"

"Of course."

She said good-bye, but Lance didn't hang up the phone. The receiver hung loosely in his hands, while he sat there, savoring the silence.

♠

"What was that?" Julia yelled, or whispered, she wasn't sure which. She didn't recognize the ceiling. Or the walls. Or the sheets. Or the . . . screaming.

Julia jumped. Her eyes sprang wide open but then cinched shut against the morning glare. She could feel her hair sticking out at odd angles from her scalp, and she could have sworn she'd eaten sandpaper during the night. All-in-all, it wasn't her best morning. Then, she remembered. Everything came back to her. Everything except—

"Helloooooooooooo!" the voice moaned again, echoing eerily through the house, and Julia bolted from the bed. She eased out onto the upstairs hallway and looked down into the Great Room, wishing Lance played golf or baseball— any sport that might result in a heavy club-like object lying around. No, of course not. She had to go and fall for the one not-sports-obsessed man on the planet. Darn him and his perfection.

She leaned over the railing, looking for Nina or Amanda, but seeing nothing. She inched down the staircase, following the reverberating screams that seemed to have gotten trapped in the cavernous space like a bird that's flown through an open window and can't find its way back out.

"Oh, hello, *helloooooo*," the scream came again, sounding like Julia was trapped in the friendliest slasher movie ever.

A cool wind blew through the open French doors as Julia eased toward the breakfast room. She saw Nina and Amanda on the patio with the ocean stretching out behind them, a glistening blue horizon, a beautiful, crystallized picture of perfection, but Julia had no sooner stepped outside than her gaze was jerked away from the Pacific and toward a ghostly figure in a white chiffon dressing gown that floated toward them as if being blown in from the sea.

"Hello!" the woman said again. Her hair was as white as her gown, and Julia might have guessed that Lance's house was haunted if the woman's high heel hadn't sunk into the damp soil of the lawn, sending her staggering the remaining three steps toward them.

"Well, hello, girls." She smiled. Her scarlet lipstick hadn't had time to bleed into the web of wrinkles that circled her mouth. Her hair looked like spun silk. Julia tried to tuck her own unruly mane behind her ears and wondered how she'd found herself in a place where even the octogenarians could make her feel ugly.

"Oh girls, is that your convertible in the drive?" the woman asked.

Nina glanced toward the driveway then said, "I guess. We rented it."

"Well, it's a doozie," the old woman said. "I used to simply *love* riding in convertibles, but with my notoriety I can't anymore. Don't want to give the vultures any more access than absolutely necessary, you know," she stated plainly. "That's why I came over—to warn you girls that you should get your gate fixed. They'll be coming through your yard to get pictures of me sunbathing on my porch."

She turned and pointed to the neighboring mansion. If Lance's house was the architectural equivalent of a Happy Meal, then this woman lived in a very high-end appetizer—small, but gorgeous and tasteful.

The woman leaned forward as she whispered, "You know, they love getting shots of us stars when we're top-less."

Amanda, Julia, and even Nina stood speechless. Amanda looked at Julia as if to say, *Long-story-short . . . gross!*, but Julia spoke first.

"It's so nice of you to come over. I'm Julia James."

"Hello, Julia." The woman held a limp hand toward to Julia, who grasped the frail fingers. "Welcome to the neigh-borhood, dear."

"Oh. No!" Julia jumped to say. "No, I don't live here. I'm just visiting. This is my friend Nina. And this is Amanda, she works for Lance Collins. *He* lives here. We're just . . ." Julia trailed off, honestly not knowing how that sentence was supposed to end. "Settling in," she said finally. "We're helping him settle in."

A light beamed from the old woman's eyes. "Oh, isn't that nice of you girls? When I saw you, I said to myself, 'Sybil, these are nice girls, you should go introduce yourself and warn them about the gate.' "

"How long have you lived here?" Nina asked, and Sybil pondered it.

"Since 1936," she said finally. "Right after I did *The Monster Mutiny* with Gregory Lane. Wonderful man," she chanted silently to herself. "Wonderful man. Always complimented me on my screams. So many others didn't, you know. They took my screams for granted."

Julia and Nina looked at each other as if they, too, knew what it was like to have your screams be taken for granted. But as Julia studied their strange new neighbor in that strange new place, she couldn't help but notice there was a sweetness in Sybil's eyes, an innocence that Julia couldn't help but respect, and Julia had to smile, feeling a little more at home. Plus, Sybil was crazy—and crazy they could handle.

Chapter Nine

A hand of gin is finished when one player knocks on the table. But even after knocking, a player can still discard one card if it doesn't help the hand.

ow's it going, kiddo?"

The voice on the phone was familiar, but strange. Julia looked out at the ocean view and tried to place her agent's Brooklyn accent within this new scene. It seemed entirely out of place. "How's my favorite author?"

"Oh, hi, Harvey."

"Now, Julia, that's no way to greet your favorite agent."

"No, I'm sorry." She felt herself starting to smile. Of course, no one could talk to Harvey without breaking into a grin. It was a reflex. It was scientific. "How are you? Are you feeling okay?"

"Darling, I'm fine. I'm fine. You don't have to worry about me. You know this old heart—it takes a lickin' and keeps on tickin'." Her agent let out a weak laugh that made him sound like the quadruple bypass survivor that he was. Every time they spoke, she listened carefully for signs that his voice was growing stronger. Maybe they were there, but in the chilly October air, Julia couldn't hear them.

"Hey, guess how many sit-ups I did today?" he said, then grew insistent. "Go ahead, guess."

Julia rolled her eyes. Well aware of the rules of the game, she said, "Forty-seven."

"Ha! Ninety-eight."

"Wow. Impressive," Julia said then teased, "But you couldn't crank out two more and make it an even hundred?"

"Tomorrow, my dear. Tomorrow." Children have received puppies and been less proud than Harvey sounded.

"That's great," Julia said, meaning it. "I'm really proud of you."

"Hey, kiddo, what's wrong? You don't sound quite like yourself."

"Oh," Julia said, sighing. "Nothing. I'm just thinking about how if I were there, you'd be daring me to punch you in the stomach as hard as I can."

"Ha!" Harvey cried. "You'd break your fist. Ha!" Harvey laughed again at his own cleverness. Then, his laughter faded. "So, how's it going?" Julia was ready for the question, though. She had her "Oh, it's . . . it's great!" right on the tip of her tongue.

"Good. Good. Glad to hear it," Harvey said, slowly, drawing out the inevitable. "You know, sweetie, I've had a few calls from people wondering if you're going to want to throw your hat back in the nonfiction ring. This Sadie Whitaker—" Julia moaned. "I know. I know," Harvey said. "But hon, the market's red hot right now because of her. And—"

"I can't write those books anymore, Harvey." Julia fingered the hem of her blouse. "I'd be . . . I don't know. I'd feel like a hypocrite or something. My fans expect certain things from me, and I . . . I just—"

"Sweetheart, it's okay," Harvey said, stepping in, sparing her from the words she couldn't say. "Hey, we're gonna set the fiction market on fire, right?"

How do you do that? Julia wanted to ask. How do you fall to a street in New York City, get rushed to the hospital, spend six hours on a bypass machine, and wake up with an unbroken heart?

"How's the house coming along?"

"Oh," Julia said. "It's fine. It's . . . Well, I'm actually in California for a few days. Visiting Lance. He bought a house, and I'm . . . visiting."

"Well, sweetheart, that's nice."

Suddenly, Julia felt like she'd been caught playing hooky. "I can work while I'm here, though. It's actually pretty good for working. I've got a . . . I think I'll have some time—"

"Julia," he cut her off as if he knew not to let her build up any momentum. "There's no rush. Why don't you enjoy yourself some? You deserve it. Lance deserves it."

"Yeah. Okay. Thanks," she said as if she needed permission.

"Yeah, this'll be good." Julia heard him smile. "You know the first thing I did when I heard you were with Lance?"

"You had a heart attack, Harvey."

"Yeah, well, after that. The first thing I did when I heard a little more about Lance was I said, 'This guy's gonna change Julia's life.'" And he had. Even Harvey was doing sit-ups. Everything was different. "Now listen up, kiddo. I want you to enjoy yourself out there, okay?"

"Absolutely."

"And sweetheart," Harvey started, choosing his words carefully, "I really don't want you getting upset by that article in *Publishers Weekly*."

What article in Publishers Weekly?

"So, Sadie Whitaker took over your spot on the Most Bankable Names in Books list. You're in a new phase of your life, and those things aren't important in the big picture. Isn't that right, kiddo?" Harvey asked, and all Julia could do was smile.

"Absolutely!" she said again.

Maybe I really do belong in Hollywood. There are Golden Globe winners who have nothing on me.

She hung up the phone. She started her computer and went back to work.

♣

"Are you sure you don't want to come?" Nina asked. "I have it on good authority they have an entire room devoted to velvet."

"Oooh. Gee. Tempting," Julia said as she glanced down at her laptop. "But I think I'll get some work done."

"Oh, yeah?" Nina asked. "Whatcha working on?" She inched forward, but Julia closed the computer as if it were top secret. It wasn't. It was just blank. Julia hadn't risen to the bestseller lists without learning to fear the empty page, but Nina didn't know this; Nina just grinned a knowing, teasing grin. "Is it about me?" she asked. "It's about me, isn't it?"

And in Nina's mind, it probably was. Julia knew that Nina was never at risk of becoming a supporting character in her own life.

As Nina stepped toward the door, Julia couldn't help warning, "You know, he hasn't officially hired you to decorate."

"Who's decorating?" Nina asked in all her wide-eyed innocence. "I'm just a concerned houseguest who is willing to make some creative suggestions."

"Suggestions that will hopefully come in under six figures," Julia said, but Nina smirked and stepped toward the doorway.

"We'll see."

Julia went back to her blank screen, her fingers feeling like cement as they perched on the keyboard ready to type should inspiration flow. But it didn't, and the screen kept on staring.

"He's gonna be here tomorrow, you know?" Julia looked up to see Nina back in the doorway, her smirk gone as she leaned around the frame.

"Yeah, I know," Julia said, trying to sound giddy, knowing giddy isn't an expression people usually aim for. It's usually one that just happens.

"Okay . . . well . . ." Nina said slowly. She took small, backward steps, inching away from the door. "You can still go with us, you know."

"Yeah." Julia smiled. "I know. I've just got—"

"Work to do," Nina finished for her as if she'd heard it all before.

"Have fun!" Julia called.

"Oh." Nina raised an eyebrow. "I will."

A few minutes later, she heard the door downstairs open and close and then the car started and drove away, and she was struck with the sound of silence. There were no hammering workmen, no humming saws, none of the sounds she had come to associate with progress, with change. She listened to the creak of the bed as she crossed her legs, the sound of the computer humming beside her. It was the soundtrack of every word she'd ever written, but she hadn't heard it in months.

She realized how, in a way, she'd missed the familiar noises, even though they'd been there all along—just drowned out somehow in the chorus of her new life.

She looked at the blank page, messed with the fonts and the margins, wondered where fonts get their names, like Times New Roman. Is that because it's what they use in the *Times* or is it because it's what they use in Rome? Or New Rome? Or when Romans read the *Times*?

These are the questions, Julia decided, that may plague man till the end of time.

She decided to check e-mail.

As she logged on to the Internet, the doorbell rang, but she didn't rush to get it. When she and Caroline were little, they had always raced to get the door. It was an honor to greet the guests, to take their coats, to offer tea. But the only people Julia knew in California had just left. And they had a key.

She clicked on the SEND-SLASH-RECEIVE icon and sat on the bed, looking at the machine that had once brought her a thousand fan letters a week. No matter how far removed from civilization she was in her small farmhouse, the outside world had always been just a click away. So she clicked.

She waited.

From: James Family Farms
To: OK Lady
Subject: Just checking on you

Julia,

It's your mother. No news here. Just checking on you. You and
Nina be careful out there (don't let her drive too fast).

Love,

Mom

P.S. When do you think you'll be coming home?

Julia read and reread the message, but she didn't write
back. *I'll call home later,* she told herself, then she clicked
SEND-SLASH-RECEIVE again, knowing that it had been only a
minute since she'd last checked, but thinking that something
wonderful might have come in those sixty seconds, knowing
that's how quickly life can change.

Then she wondered if there was an organization called
Obsessive E-mail Checkers Anonymous. If so, she probably
needed to sign up.

The doorbell rang again, and Julia clicked SEND-SLASH-
RECEIVE and felt her heart catch as the icon flashed on the
screen.

From: Beaneux Olivaradiotis
To: OK Lady
Subject: unique opportunity

Dear Sir or Madame:

My name is Beaneux Olivaradiotis and I am writing to you
from Nigeria. My situation is grave and I ask help. There are

funds that I hold which I cannot access from my country. I look
for help from trustworthy person.

"Spam," Julia said aloud. "I have officially been excited
about spam."

When her cell phone began to ring, Julia flipped it open
and said, "Hello," absentmindedly, fully expecting it to be
Nina in the middle of an ottoman emergency, but instead she
heard a familiar, "Hey."

Lance.

At the beginning of the summer, the sound of Lance's
voice would make her giddy and silly—knocking her back
at least fifteen years and fifty IQ points. But that day Julia
didn't smile, she sat up straighter and tried to pinpoint the
feeling in her gut, to understand why hearing his voice had
made her eyes burn. It was supposed to be a good thing—
wasn't it? Talking to the man you loved, the man who, by
all accounts, was crazy for you, the man who had walked
into your life and changed everything from the cardiovascu-
lar health of your literary agent to the very words you
wrote.

It was supposed to be a good thing.

"Hey," she tried, but her voice failed her and the words
never made it past her lips.

"Are you home?" he asked.

"No, I'm in California, remember?"

"That's what I mean," he said. "Are you at my house?"

"Yeah," she said. "I am. It's really—"

"Then why don't you open the door?" *Wait, has the doorbell rung since he called?* "There's a strange man there who wants to come in."

♥

A taxi sat idling by the drive, but Julia barely registered it as she stared at the man on the porch. He was thin—so much thinner than he'd looked on TV—and his hair was shorter; his clothes were new, but she found herself staring into gray eyes exactly like the ones she'd first seen nine months before.

"I don't have a key," Lance said from his side of the doorway. It sounded like an apology—like he hated to bother her by asking to be let in to his own house—like he was sorry for just dropping by. "I thought I'd have to buzz you from the gate but—"

"It's broken," she finished for him. "It's broken," she said again.

"Oh." He glanced back toward the fence just in time to see the cab leave. "I guess I could go try to fix—"

"Lance," she said, "I'm pretty sure people in this neighborhood don't fix their own gates."

"Yeah," he said as if making notes for future reference. "Right."

78

"What are you..." she started, stumbling over her words. "I mean, I thought you were coming tomorrow."

"Oh," Lance said. "Yeah. The studio had some execs coming back early and I wanted to..." He shifted, seeming nervous, looking tired. "I hitched a ride."

"Oh," Julia said, too shocked to summon any other words. *Lance is here,* she thought as she looked at him, remembering that there was a reason the silence was bothering her, that it was time for her to learn to play gin, and there was the man who had promised to teach her.

"Lance?"

"Yeah?"

"Aren't you supposed to kiss me now?"

♦

"So, what room is this?" Lance asked, but Julia thought, *Heck if I know.* It was a big square room with high windows and a huge fireplace—the same as two others on that floor, and she'd already used up living room and dining room, which only left—

"TV room?"

"Yeah," Lance said. Then he glanced at her. "Do I really need one of those?"

Julia shrugged. "I don't know. I guess it would look good with a Christmas tree in it," she said, pointing to the fireplace. "Over there."

"Okay, so this is the Christmas tree room."

"Sure." Julia nodded. "And then you can just leave the door closed eleven months a year and never take it down."

"Sounds good," Lance said as he stepped through a set of pocket doors. "Let me guess." He eyed the ornate moldings of the new space. "*Really uncomfortable furniture nobody ever sits on* room?" he said, and Julia smiled.

"Yeah, or maybe"—she looked up at the twenty-foot ceilings—"trampoline room?"

"Now *that* I might have to try."

"Yeah," Julia said. "I just wouldn't mention that idea to Nina unless you're serious about it."

They walked hand in hand into the kitchen, but Julia couldn't shake the feeling that something wasn't right. Her left hand was grasped inside his right—fingers interlaced—but that hand had never liked being held. It didn't fit with any others—never had—a simple fact that had cost her more than a few games of Red Rover.

"And this is the kitchen," Julia said, relieved to be in a room where the purpose was clear, the need was obvious.

"You sure?" he asked, gray eyes sparkling. " 'Cause that could be the world's smallest bathtub." He pointed to the sink.

It was a game she could play, she realized, dropping his hand. She opened the Subzero fridge that held three cartons of Chinese takeout and a case of Diet Coke. "Or coldest closet?"

He stepped up behind her. He circled his arms around her as the chill from the refrigerator wafted over them. Her head fell back and rested against his chest.

"I think my first apartment would have fit in there," Lance said, almost whispering the words as if he didn't realize he was saying them aloud. He looked around the rooms as if afraid that someday someone would figure out that there had been a terrible mistake somewhere—that none of that really belonged to him.

Then, he looked at Julia. "Thanks for coming," he told her.

"Thanks for being early."

When he turned again and walked away, Julia let him go. Finally he turned around and looked at her in a way that seemed to ask, *Have I made it now?* She smiled back, unable to say yes or no.

Chapter Ten

While there are many different types of rummy, some of which can accommodate multiple players, gin is a game for two.

From: James Family Farm

To: OK Lady

Subject: Hope you're okay this morning

Julia, it's your mother. Hope everything is okay there this morning.

I forgot to tell you a funny thing that happened this weekend. When little Robbie Matthews came into church he shook the preacher's hand and said, "Oh shit, I forgot my Bible."

Got to make a grocery store run later. Do you need anything from town?

Love, Mom

Y ou're the girlfriend."

It wasn't a question. The man in front of her didn't ask questions. He was Marc. Marc the publicist. Marc the PR-guru. Marc the guy who had *Entertainment To-night* on hold at that very moment. Marc. Marc. Marc, she chanted to herself, trying to think of a mnemonic device but then gave up and decided to invest in name tags instead.

Amanda was perched on Lance's granite kitchen counters, banging her sandal-covered feet against his custom cabinets, beating out a rhythm that punctuated a feel of hipness, urgentness, right-this-minuteness like Julia had never felt before. Two men passed through the arching doorway without so much as glancing her way. Another man leaned against the French doors and stared into the backyard as he held a cell phone to his ear and nodded vigorously as if the person on the other end of the conversation could see him. Every person had a purpose, a job, a task. And Julia's, evidently, was *girlfriend*.

Phones rang. Faxes hummed, and Julia was left to wonder what had happened to the big empty house from the night before. Lance had offered to take her out—to paint the town—but he was tired and she was a hermit, so instead they ordered pizza and lay on the living room floor and let Nina entertain them. Live entertainment—what could be better than that? But in the morning the house was different. It was still huge and vast, but now it was packed—full of people, full of noise. It was a factory. That was where they manufactured fame.

"Hey, sleepyhead." Lance appeared from out of nowhere and wrapped her in arms that glistened with sweat. He smelled bad. He felt good.

When she woke up that morning, she'd thought she was going to be making waffles for her best friend and the man she loved. And doing the crossword. *Sure,* Julia thought, *I know I'm new to this girlfriend business, but I'm pretty sure it's supposed to involve crosswords.* She'd even packed a little travel-sized dictionary—just in case. Then she realized she was a person who owned a travel-sized dictionary. She hung her head in shame.

"Hey, everyone," Lance said, and the room skidded to a stop. The star was about to speak. Julia glanced around the room, wondering if there was a statue of Lance with candles and burning incense that she was supposed to bow down to or something. She half expected chanting. Then Lance squeezed her shoulder and said, "This is Julia. Julia, this is . . . everybody."

Everybody stared. In that moment no cell phones rang, no faxes came, nobody even breathed as they stared, no doubt wondering what Lance Collins could possibly see in a woman who sleeps in ratty yoga pants (in which she never did any actual yoga). They were prim and professional with their cell phones and clipboards. They were taking their jobs very seriously. They were prepared to get Lance a new girlfriend by noon—all he had to do was say the word.

"Hi," Julia said as she gave the room a guilty wave, and just like that the room went from pause to fast forward.

She didn't see the other man stepping toward her until he was already extending his hand, saying, "Good morning, Julia. I'm Wes, Lance's manager. So great to finally meet you."

Is he for real? Julia wondered. She looked at him—handsome, well dressed, well spoken—a lethal combination, so she tried to hate him, to paint him with that broad brush. But when he moved, she saw an I GAVE BLOOD TODAY pin in the lapel of his jacket. It wasn't even nine o'clock and Wes had already given blood—to strangers. She wondered how much he'd give for Lance. Probably pints and pints. Needles made Julia queasy.

"If you two have a minute, we might need to talk about some things," Wes said, pulling Lance and Julia toward the small table off the kitchen—the only real piece of furniture on the entire first floor. Marc joined them, and as Julia eased into a chair, she felt like she should be wearing her good black suit and handing over a résumé—like this was the biggest job interview of her life.

Marc leaned onto the table, folded his hands together, and said, "From a PR perspective, your relationship is a little . . ." He hesitated, choosing his words carefully. Julia started to offer him use of her little dictionary but changed her mind as he said, "Ambiguous."

Ambiguous?

Then Wes leaned forward. "Lance, Julia, you two have been under the radar for a while, and tonight . . . Well, if you show up together, that's going to change." He paused a long time before adding, "We think."

They think? Julia wanted to ask. She looked at Lance. These were the experts. They were supposed to know. What did she know: ten ways to freeze lasagna in single-serving portion sizes . . . That hardly made her an expert on the Hollywood PR machine.

"It may be that people will have forgotten about your relationship and are moving on. Maybe this will stir things up," Wes said honestly.

"So we've got some decisions to make," Marc went on.

This time Lance asked, "Like what?" And Julia thought, *Under the radar. Under the radar is good, right?*

"Well," Marc began. He glanced at Wes, who returned a *go ahead* nod. "We've got to decide if we want Julia with you . . . on the red carpet."

"Oh," Julia said. "Red carpet?" She was pretty sure the red carpet was *on* the radar, a big blinking dot for all the world to see.

"Yeah," Marc said, "we need to decide if we want Lance with you on the red carpet or if you'll be meeting him inside."

Then Julia breathed again. *Inside,* she started to say, *meet him inside; please let me meet him—*

But then Lance shot forward. "What do you mean?" he asked. "Julia's with me."

"Well," Marc said, studying the suddenly quiet room, "some actors have more luck doing these things alone—not a lot of good comes out of reminding all the girls that you're taken."

He's taken, Julia thought. The words—their meaning—came from out of nowhere. Julia looked at him, and realized he wasn't protesting—asserting his independence. Lance was happy being taken . . . by *her.*

Ten feet away, Amanda was a blur of perpetual motion which, as far as Julia could see, served no acute purpose. Fingernails drummed and toes tapped. Her thin, shoulder-length hair was in a constant state of limbo, down and brushing against her tan shoulders one moment, up in a ponytail or twisted into a bun and secured by a pencil the next. Just looking at her made Julia tired.

"Well . . ." Julia started, "Lance, it's a fair point—about the fans, you know. Maybe seeing me might—"

But Lance leaned toward her. He held both her hands and spoke softly, as if the others couldn't hear, "Julia, when you were the most famous single woman in the world and I was an out-of-work actor, I didn't fake having a relationship with you so I could get a career. Now, I'm not going to fake not having one so I can keep it."

Moments before, Lance had seemed tall and straight and so at home there—so calm among the chaos. He was the eye of the tornado, the center of the storm, and right then Julia knew how scared he was of getting swept up in everything that swirled around him. In that moment they were alone again. Everything was quiet.

"But if you don't want to," Lance said then, pulling away. "If it's just"—Lance paused, choosing his words carefully—"not your scene, I guess I can—"

She reached for his hand and turned to Wes and Marc. "I'm with Lance. I'll be wherever Lance is."

"Okay," Marc said as if checking that off the list, as if he could now move on to truly important things. "We'll call your stylist and—"

"Excuse me?" Julia asked.

"You *do* have a stylist, don't you?" Marc asked.

"I . . . Of course I have a stylist."

What she had was a Nina.

Julia had always been of the opinion that a pair of black pants and an Ann Taylor sweater set could get a girl through ninety percent of the social engagements of her life, with the other ten percent being made up of things like tractor pulls and state dinners. It didn't take long for Amanda to inform her she was mistaken.

That's how she came to be squeezed inside a small shop on Rodeo Drive, and a small dressing room, and an even smaller pair of pants.

"So, Julia," Amanda said from the other side of the dressing room door. "Do you have any *people?*"

Three days before Julia wouldn't have had a clue how to answer that question. Nina was her best friend. Caroline was her sister. Madelyn and Bill were her parents, so she had people enough in her opinion but not the kind Amanda was asking about. She thought back on that morning—the crowd that followed Lance's every step—and she realized that there was absolutely no one in Julia's life who she paid to have around on a full-time basis.

"No," Julia said as she tugged on the pants, sucking her gut in and wishing the dressing room was large enough for her to lie down—something that she hadn't done to get into a pair of pants since high school, but desperate times call for desperate measures.

She jumped up and down, hoping gravity would do a lot of the work.

"So how do you, like, do it?" Amanda asked as Julia threw open the dressing room door.

"Well, for one thing, I don't buy pants that it takes two people to zip."

Amanda took a step back, cocked her head to one side, and said, "Um, maybe not."

"Ya think?" Julia snapped, feeling like a marshmallow, and not the little *put in your hot chocolate* kind—the big, whopping, *skewer them with a stick and hold them over an open flame* kind.

"Amanda," Julia said, trying to hide the disgust in her voice, which was easier than she'd thought since her current pants situation didn't exactly allow for a lot of air to enter her diaphragm, "I thought you said this store was hip-friendly."

"It is," Amanda said, eyes wide. "This place is totally hip."

Impatience boiled inside Julia. "Not hip—as in cool, as in with-it, as in last seen on the cover of *Teen Vogue*. I mean hip"—she pointed dramatically at the monstrosities the women in her family wore like a curse—"friendly."

"Oh," Amanda said, and a look filled her face as if she'd never really given any thoughts to what those curves were or why some women had them.

"Ta da!" Nina cried as she threw open the door to the neighboring stall and struck a pose. "What do you think of this?"

Only in Hollywood could Nina find clothes that were too small on her. She walked to the mirror and stood on imaginary high heels as her own reflection stared back in triplicate.

"Um, Neen, don't you think it's a little . . ." Julia struggled for words. "Tight?"

"What?" Nina asked. "No. No way." She was sizing herself up, examining all the angles.

"I think it's too tight," Julia said simply. "You won't be able to sit down."

"I won't sit."

"Your stomach's going to get all pinchy."

"I won't eat."

"Your underwear will ride up your crotch."

Nina opened her mouth to retort, but Julia instantly cut her off. "Don't say it—I don't want to hear the words come out of your mouth."

Then Julia looked around the store, and finally she couldn't hold the frustration in. The ticking of the clock on the wall seemed to echo off the hardwood floors and sparsely stocked racks as she looked at mannequin after mannequin and yelled, "Is nothing in this town A-lined?"

Nina pried herself away from the mirror and looked at her best friend.

"It's okay, Jules. We're going to find you something. Here," Nina said, holding out the first pair of pants she came to. "These are cute."

Julia snatched them and snapped, "Yes! They are cute, and I'm sure they'd look great on someone with the body of a twelve-year-old boy, but"—she stretched the pants across her body—"I'm not straight up and down. The pants are!"

Nina's eyes were wide. Amanda stared, mouth-gaping. They shared a look that signaled to Julia that they might have to join forces, call for backup, calm her down, but the panic in their eyes didn't ease Julia, it infuriated her to see them and their alliance. The skinny girls. The models and hipless wonders who could walk into any store at any time and find something—just pull it off the rack. So long as they had something smaller than a four.

Nina and Amanda didn't grow up terrified of pool parties. They'd never worn control top pantyhose under jeans. They didn't understand—no way, no how. They couldn't comprehend that there was a Hell and, right then, Julia was in it.

"Tonight is a very big thing for Lance," Julia tried to explain. "And I have to be there for him. I have to be his girlfriend. And evidently the girlfriend has to wear these pants. But I don't fit inside these pants. See." She held the pants against her one more time. "They don't fit. They just don't . . ." Her voice faded with her fury. She felt it slip away as she put the hanger back on the rack, heard the quick, cool click of metal against metal. "I guess I just don't fit."

There, Julia thought, *I've said it,* and just being free of the words made her breathe easier—the pants felt a little better.

"Julia, don't say that!" Nina cried. "It'll be okay. You're good at everything! You're . . . *you!*" And Julia realized that she might just be her best friend's hero.

"It's okay," Amanda said. "It's gonna be okay. We're gonna"—she struggled for words—"fix it."

"Yeah," Nina said.

They were nearing tears, both of them, and Julia remembered that it wasn't their fault that they'd never been held hostage by fabric and thread.

"I'm sorry," Julia said, shaking her head as if to toss everything aside and start fresh—an Etch A Sketch that had been made blank and new. "Maybe we should just—"

Just then, Julia heard a mysterious *"Psst"* coming from somewhere.

"Psst!" She heard it again.

Amanda opened her mouth to say something, but Julia silenced her with a look. "Do you hear . . ." Julia started but then a woman's face appeared in the crack of a dressing room door.

"Excuse me," she whispered. "I heard you." The woman peering out of the dressing room was tall and thin, and Julia couldn't imagine how *that* woman was going to help *her.*

Then as if reading her mind, the woman said, "I'm a stylist for . . . well . . . let's just say people you would have heard of. They're *like you*," the woman whispered as if she was describing Julia's long-lost magical ancestors, trying to make her understand that she was actually a member of a hip-wielding, paparazzi-mesmerizing, designer-defying sisterhood of women with curves.

"I have a small waist," Julia said as if that stall was a confessional and she'd finally found someone who could absolve her of her sins. "Men are *supposed* to love curves. I have a waist. I have hips. My waist is smaller than my hips!" Julia said again as if announcing it to the world.

"I know," the woman said in hushed reverence. "Jennifer Lopez doesn't buy off the rack—couldn't if she wanted to."

"I *knew* it!" Julia cried.

"There are lots of you out there. I can help."

"But I have a thing tonight," Julia said, losing momentum, but the woman waved away her fears.

"Go to this address." She placed a small slip of paper on Julia's palm then folded her fingers protectively over it. "We stylists call it"—she trailed off then looked around as if terrified she'd been caught breaking starlet-stylist confidentiality—"the hip strip. Just go." She pushed Julia toward the door. "Hurry. Tell them Angela sent you."

♣

Lance was standing by the fence, surveying the broken gate, when he heard a voice behind him.

"Hey," Amanda said. "You're not nervous, are you?"

Lance could have lied—started to, in fact. But he was tired of acting, so instead he laughed and said, "I'm terrified."

"Good. The good ones always get nervous."

"Really?"

"Totally." She sounded like an expert, so Lance was willing to take her word.

He turned back to the gate and saw where something had shorted out a fuse. The wires were fried. He could have fixed it in ten minutes if he'd had his tools, but they were somewhere else—storage . . . a box somewhere . . . a Goodwill bargain bin . . . he wasn't sure. He hadn't seen them in months, and standing there, he realized he'd probably never see them again.

"The fence guys are coming tomorrow," Amanda said.

Lance rubbed his hands together, felt the grease and dirt slide between his palms and crumble

"I put your clothes on the bed. They should fit," Amanda said. "The car's going to be here at six-thirty. Wes will ride with you. Marc's meeting us there." She looked down at the list in her hand and Lance knew, in her own way, she was a pro. "There'll be food at the party but I'm going to set some food out at six in case you're hungry and—"

"Amanda." The word was out before Lance even knew

he'd spoken it. By then, it was too late to turn back. "I was wondering if you've heard from my mom."

"Oh, well, I haven't looked at the RSVP list in a while, but—"

"That's okay," he said. "She told me she wasn't going to come, but I thought she might have changed her mind. It's nothing."

"Oh my gosh! Your mom isn't coming!"

Lance really wished he could have the past ten seconds back, but he couldn't, so instead he waved the girl away. "Really, it's no—"

"Why don't I call her and double-check? I'll go do that."

She started for the house. "No. Don't bother with it. You've already done so—"

"But I can call!" she jumped to say. "I'm sure I've got the number. Why don't I get a car service and—"

"No, Amanda. Really. It's okay."

"But it's your big night! Oh my gosh. You've got to have your family there. Oh my gosh. It's like this one time when Jodie Foster was in this movie and . . . long-story-short . . . Paraguay."

"Oh," Lance said, not really knowing what else he could say. "Wow. Yeah, it is *just* like that."

"So yes. I'm totally going to call. I'm on this!"

She turned and headed toward the house with a new purpose, but then she turned suddenly.

"I know it's none of my business"—she held her hand against her forehead, casting her eyes in shadow—"but Julia's really great, you know?"

"Yeah," Lance said. "I do know."

She nodded and smiled as if she were on to something, in the loop. "I figured."

Chapter Eleven

In gin rummy, you have to hold your cards until the end of play—laying them down mid-hand is not allowed.

s this new?"

Julia looked down at her hip-strip dress then back up at Lance. "Um . . . yeah."

"It's nice," he said then he reached for her hand. Lance was always holding her hand. For a long time she thought it was so that he could keep her from running away—like she might freak out and bolt into oncoming traffic. It took her a long time to realize he wasn't holding her back.

Then Lance turned and looked out the tinted window at lights that blurred by, landmarks Julia didn't know. She wondered if she was the only one who felt a little lost, a little dizzy.

"It's real, isn't it?" Lance asked. It was like he'd read her mind.

But before Julia could answer, Wes leaned forward and said, "It sure is, buddy. You just enjoy this. It's your night."

Lance didn't look at him, though. He looked at Julia, who nodded.

"It's gonna be great," she said. "You're going to be great."

He smiled then, as if he might believe her.

"It isn't red," Julia said. Lights flashed all around her, blinding her almost, but she held on to Lance's hand and looked down and mumbled, almost to herself, "It isn't red."

"What?" Lance asked, but Julia only glanced down at the purple carpet beneath her feet and said, "Nothing."

Purple carpet? No little girl fantasizes about flying to Hollywood and walking the purple carpet! She glanced at Lance, but he was waving toward the flashing lights. She looked at Amanda and whispered, "It's purple!"

"Smile," Amanda reminded her, pressing fingertips to dimples and then pointing toward the cameras.

Marc and Wes led the way into a tunnel of asparagus ferns. Red velvet ropes kept the photographers at bay, but they didn't stop the flashes and the screaming. She felt herself tightening her grip on Lance's hand as if she might lose him among the chaos and he'd be lost forever on that tidal wave of fame.

Screaming teenage girls called out from the bleachers. "I love you, Lance! I LOVE YOU!" And Julia saw him turn to look at her, almost asking permission to wave as a barrage of flashes filled the air, looking like fireworks through the twilight.

She felt someone come and stand beside her, and heard Wes ask, "Lance, you ready?" And then Lance looked at her in a way that seemed to ask, *Am I?*

Julia started to say something, but what she didn't know. Nothing in her life had prepared her for that moment—that man. It was just another way she didn't know how to play the game.

Lance stepped away. He smiled. He waved. Julia wanted to follow but part of her didn't know how—where that purple carpet would lead them.

"Julia," Marc said, "Lucy Knowles from that new women's cable network asked to interview you. Interested?"

"Yeah," Julia said, with one last look at Lance. "Sure."

Marc steered her toward the rope line and a tall woman with broad shoulders and arms that looked like they had never known an ounce of fat or a day away from the gym. Julia tightened the cashmere throw around her shoulders and forced a smile.

"Lucy, darling, you look magnificent," Marc said easily. He kissed her cheek then placed a hand at the small of Julia's back and pushed her closer. "Have you met Julia James? The author."

"Oh," the woman said. Her energetic grin pulled Julia closer to the rope. "I know. I'm a huge fan."

"Thank you," Julia said. She felt the pressure of Marc's hand disappear from her back, as Lucy leaned closer.

"Really, your last book kept me up all night reading it."

"The ultimate compliment," Julia said with a smile, feeling herself start to blush.

Then Lucy's eyes got wide. She pushed a microphone into Julia's face and asked, "So, is Lance going to star in the movie?"

All up and down the purple carpet, lights flashed and fans yelled and the noise seemed to reverberate in the paparazzi's tunnel-like domain, so Julia was certain she'd misunderstood.

"Excuse me?" she asked.

"Is Lance going to star when they make a movie about your book?"

Julia stared numbly at her for a moment, maybe two. Then she said, "I write nonfiction," and Lucy nodded. A second later the microphone was back in Julia's face.

"So, who's your ideal director to bring your books to the screen?"

"Thank you," Julia said, forcing a smile. "Good-bye."

And Julia turned away from the microphones and flashing lights. She spun, trying to gain her bearings on the purple carpet that was supposed to be red and continued her solitary stroll that she wasn't supposed to be making alone.

Chapter Twelve

The best gin players will always remember what they've discarded and why.

Julia sat in the dim theater as the credits rolled, trying to match the man beside her with the figure she'd just seen on the screen, but it was too surreal. How could he be there and here at the same time, a part of her wondered. Sure, it was a slightly moronic part, but the question lingered all the same. She had been to the set of *Wisdom of Solomon*. She had seen the lights and cables and fake facades that didn't make it onto the screen, and she wondered—no, she needed to know—how it could look so real. She wanted to know how Lance could bare his emotions, call on his fears and joys—put himself out there for anyone with ten bucks and two spare hours to see.

"How do you do that?" she said, thinking he couldn't

have heard. There was clapping. People were slapping him on the back, shaking his hands, but Lance leaned close.

"What?"

"How do you become someone else?"

"Julia," he said, his voice grave, concerned, "it's what I do."

There was a party in a club Julia had never heard of— that was part of its appeal, or so Amanda said. Once farm-girls from Oklahoma heard of a place, then it was time for the A-list to evacuate, jump ship, and so Julia followed Lance's entourage into a large room dimmer than the the-ater had been. On the way inside, she gripped Lance's hand.

"You were amazing. You know that, right?"

He looked down at her. He smiled.

"You say that like you're surprised." He sounded skepti-cal, cynical, and very, very pleased with himself. Standing ovations tend to do that to a guy.

"Well . . ." Julia struggled. "Yeah."

"Gee, thanks!"

"Lance," she said with a roll of her eyes, slapping his arm. "Of course I *thought* you were talented, but I'd never *seen* you before. Did you realize that? I'd never seen you act."

"Yeah," he said. "Of course I knew that. Why'd you think I was nervous?"

She looked at him, dazed. The theater had been full of studio heads and power brokers, Oscar winners, and supermodels, and yet *she* had made Lance nervous.

"What?" he asked, trying to read her face, but the room was dim and loud and he didn't know her looks yet, certainly not that one.

"Come here." And then she kissed him.

"Wow," he said when she pulled away. "I'm going to have to impress you more often, baby doll."

"Yeah," Julia said slowly. "You're also never going to call me that again. Right?"

He quickly looked away. "Of course not."

A moment later, Wes was at Lance's side. "Sorry to interrupt, guys, but Julia, I'm going to need him for a minute if it's okay. The head of the studio is four drinks into a twelve-drink night and history has taught me you want to catch him somewhere between three and seven."

"Go," Julia said.

But Lance held on to her hand as he stepped away. "I want to just—"

"I'm fine," she insisted, letting go, but still he held on. "Go be famous or something."

Wes was tugging at Lance's other side, and he couldn't fight them both.

◆

"So," Nina said, appearing beside her. In her tight red pants she looked remarkably like a little devil perched on Julia's shoulder. "Miserable yet?"

Julia looked at her, shocked. She was at the hottest party in Hollywood. She was with the hottest guy at the hottest party. She was wearing a hip-friendly dress. "Nina, why would I be miserable?"

"No offense," Nina said before Julia could say anything. "I just know how you don't like people."

"That's ridiculous," Julia snapped.

"Ridiculous"—Nina raised an eyebrow—"but true."

Then Julia glanced around the massive room. People stood in circles, drinks in hand. Waiters floated through carrying trays of food that no one ever ate. Cheeks were kissed. Hands were held. Compliments were given and all Julia could do was watch, wide-eyed, as she realized, *Oh crap! I am miserable*. Then she glanced at her best friend and said, "I *used* to like *you*."

"Everybody likes me," Nina said, pulling an hors d'oeuvre from a passing tray. "I'm contagious . . . like chicken pox . . . but in a good way."

Photographers roamed freely as if they worked for *National Geographic*, and every once in a while a flash would go off, brightening the dim room like a bolt of lightning in the night.

"Hey, Jules," Nina said faintly, "do you think my husband might be here?" She wasn't being sarcastic or funny. She seriously wanted to know because Nina believed in soul mates. Nina believed in big, lose-yourself, only-happens-in-movies love. Nina had been asking herself that very question since the second grade when she'd looked around Mrs. Nichols's classroom and found Jason. And now, so many years later, Nina was still looking. Julia knew she'd never stop.

"What do you think of him?" Nina asked, gesturing to a tall man a few feet away. "Or him?" A waiter offered champagne to a group of women in the corner. One probably made six-fifty an hour and the other six figures a year. Nina was nothing if not equal-opportunity-desperate.

"*I* love you, Neen," Julia said. "You know that, right?" But Nina didn't seem to hear, and Julia wondered if she'd ever heard those words and if she ever believed them.

"Oh, he is cute," she said when a man passed by who bore an eerie resemblance to Jason—West Coast Jason, Prada-suit Jason.

"Nina, you—"

But Nina was spinning, draining her drink in one long gulp. "Are you going to mingle or are you going to stand here by yourself being miserable?"

Sometimes Julia thought she needed therapy. Then she remembered, she had Nina. And there was no sense paying someone three hundred bucks an hour to find out what Nina already knew—that you could give Julia a stage and a microphone and she could entertain a thousand people. Put her on national TV and she could sell a million books. Just don't give her a drink and a cocktail napkin and ask her to make small talk at a party.

"Mingle," Julia said, swaying a little too much, smiling a little too broadly. "I'll *totally* mingle."

♠

Three hours later, Julia was standing alone in a dark corner, waiting for midnight so the chariot would turn back into a pumpkin and everyone could just go home. The ice sculpture had lost its shape and now sat like a glob in a pool of chilly water. Julia watched it drip, drip, drip away as she realized that maybe the fairy tale night was over—that even with the perfect dress, glass slippers are still murder on your feet.

"Excuse me?" someone said, and Julia turned around and saw a woman inching her way, so Julia leaned back against the wall and quickly practiced the four answers she'd given to the two hundred questions she'd already been asked.

Yes, I am Lance Collins's girlfriend.

No, I won't show him your screenplay.

Yes, I am very proud.

No, I can't introduce you to his agent.

"Excuse me, but aren't you Julia James—the author?" the woman asked.

But in that second, Julia didn't know the answer. Instead,

she stood on the outskirts of the party, trying to place the woman who had found the shadows, too. Finally, Julia remembered to nod even if she couldn't find the words to answer.

A bright smile stretched across the woman's face as she said, "I thought so." Then she waved her hands as if to explain, "I recognized you from your author photo."

Julia couldn't believe her ears. She bolted forward.

"You've read my books?"

"Of course!" the woman cried in a very *don't-be-silly* tone. "I use *Spaghetti and Meatball* every day. Every day! Your recipe for Uno Enchiladas alone has *saved* my *life*." The woman laughed, and Julia joined her; it was such an infectious sound, completely free of pretension. "As you can probably tell by looking at me."

She placed her hands on her midsection, and Julia contemplated telling her about the hip strip, but before she could say a word, the woman was leaning closer. When she spoke, the laughter was gone. "When I got divorced, a friend of mine gave me *Table for One*. I know it wasn't about divorce, per se, but it helped." She nodded as if that was something she had needed to say for a very long time. "It really helped. So, thank you for that."

Julia had met women like this before—thousands of them. They wrote her letters. They stood in lines and posed beside her for pictures. In that moment Julia caught a glimpse of her old life. It was as if she were flipping through a photo album and came to a page she'd forgotten. Memories that brought a smile to her lips.

"So when the girl in the bathroom asked if I knew you, I just had to . . ." The woman trailed off then threw one hand to her lips in horror. "Oh no. I forgot. I'm terrible."

No, you're a saint!

"There's a girl in the bathroom who was looking for you." *Nina?* Julia instantly stood on her tiptoes and began scanning the crowd.

"Oh," the woman said, biting back a chuckle. "No, I think she needs you to go find her—in there."

Definitely Nina.

♣

"Go ahead," Nina said when Julia joined her in the stall. "Say it. I know you want to." She paused, trying to will the tears back into her eyes as she put on a brave face and said, "I deserve it."

But Julia didn't say, *I told you so.*

"Don't laugh!" Nina pleaded, but it was too late. Julia couldn't help herself. Laughter exploded out of her—it wasn't her fault. The laughter was a beast and it had to be set free. It wasn't nervous laughter. It was *someday you'll agree this is funny* laughter. She roared until she had to use toilet paper to dab at her tearing eyes. She bellowed until she had to lower the lid on the toilet and sit down, but from that angle she was directly in front of the crotch of Nina's pants, which had split wide open. Julia laughed harder as she said a silent prayer that, at least, Nina had worn underwear—hot pink Hello-Kitty underwear, but underwear just the same.

She dabbed at her watering eyes with toilet paper until the laughter subsided. Then she exhaled and sighed. "That felt good."

"Julia!" Nina cried, sounding on the verge of tears. Real tears. "What am I going to do?"

She was bouncing, vibrating as if she really, really had to go to the bathroom—except they were *in* the bathroom. So, Julia placed a hand on her arm, and said, "Tell me what happened." Then Julia glanced down at the seam that was totally gone—the gash that ran almost from waistband to waistband—and Julia retracted her question. "Never mind."

"Julia! What am I going to do?" Nina cried again, bouncing up and down on the balls of her feet. "Thank GOD I was close to the bathroom when . . ." She looked down. "I thought I could just sit down a little bit . . . you know . . . if I slouched. And then I heard it; and I felt it; and I bolted in here."

"Nina, calm down. It's going to be—"

"Julia!" Amanda's voice called. "Are you—"

Julia peeked her head out, saw they were alone, then swung the door wide for Amanda to see.

"Oh my gosh!" the girl gasped. She threw her hands into

the air. "Oh my . . . Oh my . . . Oh . . ." Then she sighed. She perched her hand on her hip and said, "Oh Nina, it's okay. Like I remember this one time, Oprah was doing this special and . . . long-story-short . . . Gwyneth Paltrow."

Nina's eyes went wide. "Did you hear that, Jules? I'm like Gwyneth Paltrow."

Nina was exposed, humiliated, but in her mind she was just like Gwyneth Paltrow. How was Julia supposed to make *her* feel better?

"Julia?" Amanda said. "When . . . you know . . . you can, Lance is looking for you."

"Sure," Julia said. She glanced around the empty bathroom while music and laughter seeped in from the other room. She took the cashmere wrap from her own shoulders and wrapped it around Nina's waist. "There," Julia said.

Nina stepped in front of the mirrors, spinning, examining the effect of the flittering fringe. Then she stopped suddenly, struck a pose, and said, "Let's party!"

She stepped toward the door as if five minutes before the world according to Nina hadn't been about to end. As she joined step with Amanda and they pushed through the doors, Julia realized that Nina was always bursting at the seams. There wasn't any room in her small body for excess, so whatever she was feeling at the moment spilled out, bubbled over. Her cup was perpetually full.

"There you are," Julia said to Lance when she finally found him. He was standing against the wall at the far side of the room. He seemed almost barricaded, and she imagined she was saving him from some mindless industry drone who was pitching a project, pushing an idea. Half out of breath, she said, "Sorry to interrupt"—she spoke to the man beside him and then turned back to Lance—"but Nina's had a little . . . thing . . . and we're going to grab a . . ."

But her gaze flew back to the other man as she saw it— the similarity. Slowly, Julia looked between Lance and the man who stood beside him, and she felt as if she was seeing the future. Gray fringed his temples; character lined his face. It was Lance in thirty years, and Julia went mute at the sight of him. After all, it's one thing to meet a male icon-slash-Academy Award winner. It's quite another when he's your boyfriend's father.

"Julia," Robert Wells beamed. His strong hand grasped her own. "My dear, I feel like I know you."

But Lance only turned his head. He spoke under his breath to the shadows in the corner of the room. "That makes one of us you know."

Julia turned on him; she felt her mouth part to speak, but in that moment she didn't see the man she loved. She saw a little boy instead, a very little boy who has vowed to hate someone forever.

"I was just talking to Lance." Robert gestured toward his son with his drink. Then he turned, scanned the crowd, and said, "Actually, I was also hoping to say hello to your mother."

"It's not her scene," Lance said. The words were hard—bitter. Julia stared numbly at him, words failing her, not sure whether she should scold or console. She might have stood like that forever if one of the roaming photographers hadn't appeared and said, "Oh, great, father and son," in that cheery *every-moment-is-a-memory* voice that people with cameras seem to always have.

Julia wanted to do something, say something, but she knew she couldn't cause a scene—that would be the worst possible thing to do at that moment, so instead she lunged between Lance and the photographer, grabbing the young man's shoulder and spinning him to where Nina stood, ten feet away, waiting for Julia to say her good-bye.

"Look! Nina Anders!" she said as if she knew something the photographer didn't, and it worked. The flash burst, blinding everyone within ten feet in any direction.

When she turned around again, both Lance and his father were gone.

Chapter Thirteen

> If you are going to win at gin, you'd better have a very good memory.

W hat time is it?" Julia asked as Nina dealt.

"Five seconds after the last time you asked," Nina said.

She kept thinking about Lance's face as he stood in the shadows, avoiding his father's eyes. She remembered Wes's words in the limo home, the way he'd touched Julia's arm as she started to crawl out of the car and said, "Take care of our boy, okay?" as if he knew—as if he'd seen it, too, so Julia didn't want to pick up her cards. She fingered the backs, traced the image she knew so well, and tried not to think about what lay on the other side.

"Hello!" Nina chimed. "Your turn."

They were alone in that huge mansion, fifteen hundred miles from home, but they might as well have been on her bed, in her house. Sometimes it doesn't matter how far or fast you run.

"What time is it?" Julia asked again.

"Maybe it's somebody's bedtime."

Then Julia spun to look at the clock herself. The green numbers glowed atop the microwave. A quarter past two.

"Lance is a big boy," Nina said as she fanned the cards out in her hand. "Besides, how hot was Lance's dad, huh? Wow!" She scanned her cards, pulled out a three of clubs, and tossed it to the top of the pile. "He's totally going to look like that when he gets older, you know—hot like that. He's totally going to—"

"Nina?" Julia asked. "Can I ask your advice about something?"

Nina nearly dropped her cards. "Does this relate to ottomans?" she asked, but Julia shook her head. "Color palettes? Automotive maintenance or achieving maximum acceleration?"

"No," Julia said simply. "Divorce."

Then Nina rearranged her hand a little. She fanned her cards again—made them perfect—and slowly said, "Yeah. On *that*, I am an expert."

It was just another way that they were opposite—another example of how Nina's life had zigged when Julia's life had zagged. Nina liked to joke that she was always a bride, never a bridesmaid, but Julia knew Nina's real expertise ran deeper, went back further.

"Do you ever want to see your mom?"

Julia could tell that she'd surprised her; which was strange—usually the surprises flowed in the other direction. Julia wasn't used to being the wild card. But it was something she had to ask. Something she had to know.

After all, Julia had never met Nina's mother. She was gone long before the day in second grade when the tiny girl claimed the desk next to Jason's. But Nina's mother was everywhere, somehow, like a ghost that lingered long after the casseroles she'd left in the freezer were gone. Even after thirty years, Nina still got nauseous at the sight of tuna.

Nina dropped her cards to the table. "I used to."

"But you don't now?"

"No."

"Why?"

She turned to her then, and Julia saw something she'd seen on her best friend's face only once or twice before. Frailty.

"Because it's been too long."

Julia wanted to ask more, to understand. But there are buttons you shouldn't push, doors you shouldn't walk through, so she let her best friend go upstairs. So she said her good night.

The cards lay in front of her for a long time, tempting her, but Julia didn't shuffle. She might have reached for them, might have broken down, if she hadn't heard the cab drive up, if Lance's key hadn't turned in the lock.

"Hey," she said, rushing toward him. "How are you? Are you . . ." But she couldn't finish because he pulled wordlessly away and started up the stairs. Julia followed. He was more than the man she loved then, he was a mystery she needed to solve.

When Julia appeared in the bedroom doorway, Lance was pulling his shirttails out of his pants and then fumbling with the buttons in the manner of a man who is unused to his own hands.

"Go ahead," he said. "Ask."

She took a step toward him. "What happened? Did you talk? Did you . . ." She wanted to say *work everything out*, but he cut her a look that said she should quit while she was ahead.

Then Lance looked away. His shoulders slumped and his defenses fell.

"Robert Wells," Lance said slowly, "is a very good actor."

"I know," Julia said, moving closer.

"Actors make great liars." His shirt was open, and Julia feared a strong wind could carry him away, but when he sank to the bed, she felt a mountain of worries descend with him onto the sheets.

She wanted to know why he didn't talk to her—was it something he couldn't say, or was it just something he knew she wouldn't understand? Right then she cursed her loving parents and happy childhood. They'd never prepared her for this.

"I'm sorry I'm so late, Julia. I'm sorry you were worried. I just . . . I needed a little time alone."

"But your dad? You left with—"

"No. He left." Lance pulled off one shoe and dropped it. She heard the sharp crack as Italian leather struck hard wood, and something about it sent a shiver down her spine. "It's something he's really good at."

"Lance, I—"

Then he looked at her as if he were seeing her for the first time. "You were the only person there tonight who knew me nine months ago. Did you know that?"

Julia shook her head.

"You're the only one who had faith in me before they knew about him."

"Lance, that's not true. I bet your mother—"

"But my mother wasn't there." He looked down, as if he couldn't face her as he asked, "Was she?"

He eased down onto the pillow, half-dressed, and Julia lay down beside him.

His arm fell around her waist. His warmth seeped into her back.

"I'm sorry," Lance whispered.

"I'm not," she whispered back.

The house was dark around them, quiet and still and a thousand miles away from the screaming fans and flashing cameras, but Julia lay awake for a long time, listening to him breathe. Waiting for the other shoe to drop.

Chapter Fourteen

It's best to remember, but not dwell on, the cards in the discard pile. Once discarded, a card is probably gone forever.

From: James Family Farm

To: OK Lady

Subject: Hope you had a nice time last night

I hope you girls enjoyed the show last night. Dad said he might take me when the movie opens here, since we know the star.

I'll guess you'll be coming home now, won't you? Just let us know if you need someone to pick you up at the airport.

Tell Lance we're very proud and that I've got some huckleberries in the freezer I'm saving just for him.

Love, Mom

t was almost noon the next day before Julia heard the crying.

"Amanda," Julia said and knocked. Then, she tried the knob.

She peered inside and saw the girl sitting on the edge of a bathtub, wiping her eyes with toilet paper still attached to the roll.

"Amanda, what's wrong?"

The girl glanced toward Julia, and even though Nina was the only other person in the house, Julia closed the door. Amanda nodded as if thanking her for the privacy, as if asking her to come inside.

Her big blue eyes were swollen and her bottom lip quivered as if she didn't dare let loose of all her grief—holding some in for good measure.

"Julia, I'm gonna ask you a question, and you've got to tell me the truth. Okay?" Amanda said, voice breaking and cracking under the strain. "Because we're friends, right?"

"Well . . ." Julia stammered, unsure what to say. After all, she'd really only just met Amanda, and in Julia's experience friendship was a big step—one that sometimes involved furniture moving and shower throwing—and Julia wasn't sure she was ready to make that kind of commitment. But when she looked at the girl's puffy blue eyes, all Julia could do was say, "Sure. Yeah. Of course we're friends!"

Amanda pulled on the toilet paper, and a fresh piece rolled toward her. She blew her nose.

"So you'd tell me if Lance . . . *hates me*?"

And then the holding in became too much for her. The

dam broke and the tears ran free, so Julia did the only thing she knew to do—she pulled on the toilet paper, sending the roll spinning, shoving white cottony clouds toward Amanda's gushing eyes.

"Ooh," Julia said. "Don't cry. Don't . . . Oh . . ." She tugged on the roll again, and when Amanda paused to catch her breath, Julia jumped to say, "Of course Lance doesn't hate you. Why would you think that? Why would—"

"It's just that yesterday was *sooooo* crazy, and now Wes is *sooooo* mad and he *sooooo* should be. And I know it's all my fault. And I'm sorry. I really, really am," Amanda said through her sobs. "And I know it was a mistake. It's just—"

"Amanda, what is wrong?" Julia said, trying to force it out of her.

"He just seemed so worried about having his family there, and I know it was a big night and . . . long-story-short . . . *I* invited his father."

She blew her nose again and kept pulling on the toilet paper, pull after pull until a pile formed in the center of the bathroom floor. Her sobs echoed in the small space.

"I didn't know. I swear. He asked me to check on whether or not his mom was coming, so while I was at it, I checked on his dad. I didn't know, Julia. I swear. I thought . . . I just need to know if Lance hates me."

No, Lance doesn't have it in him to hate, Julia wanted to say, but she knew differently now. He did hate. Of course he did. He was human, and for the first time, Julia was starting to see it. She just wasn't sure if she liked it.

"I knew it!" Amanda cried, confused by Julia's silence, and then she erupted in tears.

"No, Amanda," Julia said, easing down beside her on the edge of the tub, realizing that the comforting-mothering-consoling stuff was Caroline's territory. Julia gave Amanda's back two awkward *there, there* pats and said, "Amanda, no. I'm sure he doesn't hate you. He was just mad, that's all. He's just not . . . *good* where his father is concerned."

"See!" Amanda said then, brightening. "I didn't know that. I'm supposed to know that." She leaned closer to Julia, confiding, whispering despite their solitude, "Assistants are supposed to know *everything*."

So are girlfriends, Julia thought.

Julia sat there, rubbing Amanda's back in slow, awkward circles like she'd seen her sister do, but not drawing any comfort from it. She thought about the things she knew: the facts she could find or read on about a hundred Lance Collins websites—that his father rose to fame; that his mother managed small community theater companies; that Lance didn't use his father's name. Those were the facts, but Julia never talked about them in the way she tried never to discuss things she didn't fully understand—like politics and world trade. She was content to focus on the big picture.

"Wes wanted to *fire* me," Amanda said, moaning slightly

as the tears came faster. "But Lance . . ." She rubbed her face with her sleeve. "Lance said it was okay. But it wasn't—you know—okay. He was really upset. I really, really blew it." Julia could imagine someone warning her she'd never pick up dry cleaning in that town again.

"Oh, no, Amanda," Julia lied. "It wasn't a big thing. The movie was a big hit. That's all anyone really cares about. That's all Lance cares about—I'm sure. It's okay."

"It is?" Amanda said, questioning at first then growing certain. "Of course it is! I won't ever mess up like that again."

"No. No you won't," Julia soothed.

"Because you're going to help me."

"I am?" Julia asked, then added, "Of course . . . yes . . . I am."

"And you know Lance better than anyone."

There was a gas station just inside the Park Valley city limits, so Lance stopped and got directions, even though he was pretty sure he wouldn't need them. Without being told, he knew the state highway would turn into Main Street; he knew the theater would be downtown, and he'd find it on his first pass through. He parallel parked and walked to the doors, and even though he'd never been there before, he knew exactly what he was going to find inside.

As he pushed the door open, white light from outside swept across the dim theater, over threadbare red velvet seats. Lance took off his sunglasses and waited for his eyes to adjust. Everything smelled like mothballs and wood polish. Three women stood around the base of a ladder at stage left, and the acoustics in the old building carried their voices all the way to the door.

"Roger, more to the left," one of the women said. She was wearing a pink velour tracksuit from when velour was in style the first time. It was activewear. She was being active. And yet, Roger was the one up there on the ladder.

"No, the other left," another woman said.

Roger had a thick stomach and thin hair. Lance's guess was that his wife had been dead eighteen months. The women looked up at him longingly. Roger was quite a catch.

To Lance's right, a pair of girls kneeled beside three pieces of poster board, sprinkling glitter over glue-covered letters that said tickets would be five dollars each—just like they must do it on Broadway. Strands of long, fine hair fell over their faces, shielding Lance from their view as he stepped toward them and said, "Hi. Excuse me."

They looked up at the same time and their hair fell back as, simultaneously, their jaws dropped.

"*Ohmygosh,*" one of them said in a breathless whisper.

"Hi. I'm Lance, and I think my mom might be—"

"Ohmygosh!"

As they stumbled to their feet, Lance could see that one was tall and shapely, while the other carried twenty more pounds on three fewer inches. The taller one shook her hands as if her fingers were on fire. "OH! MY! GOSH!!!"

On the stage, someone said, "Be careful, Roger," but the girls were bouncing up and down then, grasping each other, screeching at the top of their lungs, and Lance didn't know what do to.

Fans, he thought. *I guess these are fans.* Like most forces of nature, they looked different up close, in their native habitat.

"I love you," the heavier girl cried. "I love you so much!"

But you don't even know me, Lance thought but couldn't say. Lance pulled his hand back and gestured toward the stage, where Roger was moving the ladder and the women watched his butt as he climbed. Right then, Lance was really, really glad he wasn't Roger.

"You're doing *A Christmas Carol*?" Lance asked, but the girls were speechless. He pointed to himself and said, "You're talking to a former Tiny Tim—five years running."

"He's not tiny anymore," the taller girl whispered to her friend.

While they giggled, Lance stepped toward the stage and said, "Is my mom—"

"Yeah, she's in the prop room. I can take you—" The girl gestured backstage and motioned for him to follow, but Lance said, "Oh, thanks, but I can find it."

He tried hard not to hear the squeals and giggles that followed as he walked away.

The door was open, so he stood in the hallway for a second, watching. She held a piece of red velvet in her hands and worked a needle and thread through the fabric with such practiced ease, Lance almost watched in awe. As a boy, he'd thought there was nothing his mother couldn't do. She could turn a stage in the deserts of Arizona into an island in the South Pacific; she could make an aging homecoming queen look like Cleopatra. She could convince junior high school vice principals and deputy chiefs of police that they should run away to New York and try their hand at the Great White Way. He'd always thought that was typical—that all kids grow up thinking their mothers sewed by hand the reality in which they lived.

"Are you going to help me, or are you going to stand out there all day?" She hadn't turned around. She never missed a stitch.

"Hey, Mom," he said as he stepped inside and hugged her from behind.

"Pull up a seat."

He looked around the cramped space filled with boxes

and mannequins and finally eased down onto an overturned milk crate.

"You look good," he said, and it was true. He wondered if she had some secret, but if she did, she'd never tell, would never admit to needing or wanting such a thing, so instead he just said, "*A Christmas Carol*?"

She rolled her eyes. "*A Christmas Carol*. Don't suppose you're free December second through the fourteenth—our Tiny Tim doesn't look very healthy to me and the chicken pox has been going around. We could use an understudy."

Lance grinned. "I'll check with my agent."

"Good. Tell him he can have fifteen percent of all the food you eat at the cast party."

"I'll do that."

She put her needle into the padded cuff she wore on her wrist, folded the velvet carefully, and pulled a gauzy dressing gown from the pile beside her. She held it to the light—looking for holes.

"The last time I checked, L.A. was a good three-hour drive from here," she said.

"Can't a guy come see his mother?"

She looked back down at the fabric in her hands. "I'm sorry I wasn't there for you last night, darling. I know now I should have—"

"Dad came."

Her hands stopped moving, but her gaze never left the fabric. "And . . ."

"I hadn't seen him in six years, and that's when he shows up."

She flapped the gauzy fabric out in front of her. "You've made it a point not to see *him* in six years. I don't know why, Lance. Those are your issues. Your feelings toward your father are—"

"I want you to tell him to stay away from me."

"You need him more than me now, Lance," she said. "You don't know it, but you do. And he loves you—you don't know it, but he does."

Outside, somebody laughed and Lance wondered what that felt like, and realized in that moment he'd forgotten. He stood to leave but found himself stuck in the doorway, held there by a magnetic combination of the woman behind him and that old theater. It was the closest Lance could come to going home.

Chapter Fifteen

People who consistently win at gin always know what the other player needs.

Lance walked into the house, wanting it to be empty, needing to slip upstairs and take a nap and forget everything for a while, but Julia was sitting on the stairs, holding a pack of papers that were joined together by a single staple. She didn't look at him as she flipped through them, studying the pages.

"Hey, what are doing down—"

"Do you like chocolate ice cream?"

The way she spoke, the way she looked, he expected her to be telling him that she only had six months to live, but instead she just said, "I don't know what kind you like. Amanda asked me to fill this out, but I don't know . . . Is chocolate okay? I put down chocolate."

"I'm on low-carbs right now, Julia. I can't have ice cream."

"I didn't know that," she said as if apologizing. She looked down at the list in her hands and started to write something in. "See, I didn't know that." But Lance took the pen from her hands. He sank to the step beside her.

"Julia, what's wrong?"

"I don't know this one either," she said, pointing to another line on the list. "Allergies? This one's pretty important. This one could lead to hospitalization or—"

"What is that?" Lance pulled the papers from her hands.

"Amanda made it," Julia said. "She feels awful about last night and wants to make sure she doesn't mess up again."

"I'm not mad at Amanda," Lance said then paused, wishing he could stop having different versions of the same conversation, wishing the scene would change. "Last night was"—he shook his head, searching for words—"inevitable. She doesn't have to worry about this stuff." Lance pulled the papers from Julia's hand. "You don't have to worry about this stuff." He wanted to crumble them in his fist and toss them into the trash. Two points. But then he scanned the sheets of paper. "Julia, she asked how long we've been dating and you put a question mark."

"I didn't know what to put." She shrugged. "We never have dated—not really. We just *were* all of a sudden." She stood and took a step down the stairs, away from him. "If you want to be technical about it, we never dated."

Lance had never thought about it like that. Somehow, to him, they had begun that first day in New York when he'd lied his way into a restaurant and into her life—like a blind date neither of them knew they'd been set up on. He'd even given her flowers. What else was a guy supposed to do?

But then he looked at Julia, recognized something in her, something he hadn't seen in a long time, but he knew had been there, simmering underneath. He saw the woman he'd first met—the beautiful woman who hated how she looked, then remembered how easy it would be for her to pull away, how much she had to go home to, that he was the only reason she had to stay.

"Hey, Julia," Lance called out to her. She turned and rubbed her hands on her jeans. "Wanna go on a date with me?"

The smile that spread across her face started slowly, like the sun rising—little rays of it that came first and then grew into a full-on glare. It was so easy, he realized, making her smile. He vowed to do it more often.

"Tomorrow night?" he asked.

"Sure. Tomorrow night."

She took another step. "And Julia," he called, and she turned back. "I love chocolate ice cream. Chocolate ice cream is perfect."

Chapter Sixteen

> After the deal is complete, the deck is placed in the center of the table so it is accessible to all the players.

From: James Family Farm

To: OK Lady

Subject: We sure could use a rain

> It's getting really dry. We sure could use a rain.
>
> How's the weather there?

Love,

Mom

Y ou're not gonna wear your hair like that, are you?" Nina asked.

"What's wrong with my hair?" Julia wanted to know.

Nina shrugged. "I don't know. It's just not very *first datey*."

"Don't you two have something to accessorize or something?"

"Sure," Nina said. "You."

Forty-five minutes later, Julia was sitting on a closed toilet seat while Amanda said, "Stop twitching," every time Nina burned Julia's ear with the curling iron. Still, Julia couldn't hold still.

"You do realize I'm in my mid-thirties, don't you?" Julia asked. "It's not the prom. Ouch!"

"If you'd stop moving, I'd stop burning you," Nina chided, passing the blame. Then she turned to Amanda, who sat perched on the vanity, wearing every necklace the three of them owned, a human display rack primed for the picking. "Where's he taking her?" Nina wanted to know.

"I can't say." Amanda sounded proud of herself—in the know. She wasn't going to sing no matter how hard Nina put the screws to her. She was through making mistakes.

"Oooh!" Nina practically squealed as she jumped up and down and clapped. "This is so romantic. I want to come!"

Julia knew that Nina tagging along would obviously make it less romantic—a whole lot less—but for a second she contemplated it—a guide, a coach . . . backup.

Nina grabbed another section of hair and twirled it around the hot iron.

"Not too big," Julia reminded her.

"It'll be okay," Nina said. "It'll fall."

"No, it won't!" Julia warned. After all, she was a big-haired girl from the world capital of big-haired girls. Her hair knew better than to fall; falling was for the hair of amateurs.

"Come on, Amanda," Nina said, all pouty, "tell us where he's taking her," and Julia started to suspect then that the real reason Nina wanted to know was so that she and Amanda could follow. And wear trench coats. And hide behind ferns and really big menus. They'd have top-secret rendezvous in the ladies' room when they'd decide, as a committee, whether Julia should order the soup or salad with her entrée. Knowing Nina, there might have even been walkie-talkies involved.

But Amanda cinched her lips together then twisted her thumb and forefinger in the corner of her mouth—turning the key. Then, as if that wasn't good enough, she threw the key away. *How are you ever going to eat again?* Julia wanted to cry. They were going to have to feed Amanda through a tube thanks to her relentless devotion to her job! But then Julia remembered that Amanda never ate.

"Well," Nina said, "just as long as he has her home by midnight."

♠

"I believe we have a—"

"Reservation. Yes," the maître d' said, pulling together

two menus before Lance could even say his name. "Follow me."

Lance looped an arm around Julia's waist and ushered her in front of him. The heat of his hand burned through her dress. She felt both protected and like property. She could follow a maître d' by herself, couldn't she? And yet that hand was there, guiding her, steadying her, reminding her that she wasn't walking alone, that someone else cared where she ended up, so Julia stumbled—not intentionally—but he caught her just the same.

"Ma'am," the maître d' said as he held a chair and gestured for Julia to sit down. The maître d' handed them their menus and was gone.

They'd walked through the dim restaurant onto an outdoor patio. The ocean lapped in the distance, and the moon fell in rippling light across the waves.

"Oh my gosh," Julia said without meaning to.

"What?" he asked.

"Oh." She felt embarrassed, uncool. "Nothing."

"No," he reassured her. "What?"

"It's just . . ." She leaned closer and whispered, "I just realized we're alone."

He glanced around the dim patio. They weren't really alone. A man, woman, and teenage girl sat in the far corner. The woman kept looking at the menu and then turning to scan the courtyard as if, at any minute, someone was going to figure out they didn't belong there and drag them away to a Red Lobster or an Olive Garden. The man kept insisting on raising his glass and saying, "To Stanford," every few minutes, so either the girl was college-bound or someone named Stanford had made quite an impression. In any case, his wife really wished he'd shut up.

But Julia doubted that Lance had even noticed. He was too busy looking at her, staring really. Finally she cocked her head and raised her eyebrows until he blurted, "How have you been? Has it been okay? Are you okay? Is this awful for you?"

"Yes," Julia said. "This is most women's idea of torture. In fact, I think the moonlit dinner with a movie star treatment was banned by the Geneva Convention if I'm not mistaken."

"Julia, seriously." He lowered his voice. He leaned closer. "I know I haven't been around much, and the house is a mess, and there are all these crazy people. And I'm crazy, and . . . It's gonna get better."

She pulled her hand away and smoothed the napkin over her lap. She didn't want to touch him then. She didn't want him to feel her pulse race when she said, "I know." She found his eyes and smiled. "I know."

"Excuse me."

Julia turned to see a woman holding a young girl by the shoulders in front of her—like a human shield. "Excuse us,

Mr. Collins, but my daughter was wondering if she could have your autograph." The girl held out a slip of paper and a pen, and Lance smiled and nodded. He was a perfect combination of accommodating and reserved. He was a saint. He was a movie star. Then his eyes cut to Julia and a boyish grin flashed over his face—part apology, part *can you believe this is happening to me*. He was so darn cute that Julia wanted to pinch herself—or better—pinch him.

When the woman and the girl were gone, Lance said, "You said I'd get used to that," as if his blushing cheeks were all her fault.

"When did I say that?" she asked.

He looked at her. "The day we met. Remember? We were at the toy store and that woman wanted your autograph, and you said, 'You'll get used to it.' "

But Julia didn't remember. She tried to recall just one of the thousands of times in her life when someone asked for her autograph, but she drew a blank. She wondered if Lance was one of those freaks who can remember everything that ever happened to him—like maybe he could recount in detail what he wore on the first day of second grade or something. But no, she realized. He just remembered the important stuff, and that moment had been important to him long before it was important to her. Lance had had a head start on loving her.

Suddenly, the plate in front of Julia became very, very

interesting—like it was the most important plate in the world or something—and she found herself saying, "I love salad."

"Okay . . ." Lance said, half-laughing.

"Really," she jumped to say. "I do, but I never used to eat them, because you know, the good lettuce—the kind in the bags—goes bad so soon after you open it." He looked at her like she was crazy. "It does!" she said, defending her stance. "I even wrote about it in *Spaghetti and Meatball*, about how if you put paper towels in the bag, it lasts longer. And then I thought the bag salad people would wise up and start making smaller bags, or bags sealed in the middle, you know, so you only have to open half and then . . ." She trailed off when she realized he was staring—that he wasn't laughing anymore.

"You were really good at being single. Weren't you?"

Julia looked at him. "Well, yeah," she said. "I guess I was."

He took a deep breath. She felt like maybe an ex-boyfriend or fiancé had just walked in the room carrying a Harvard diploma and a Super Bowl ring and a Nobel Peace Prize. He looked like he'd never be able to compete with her thoughts on lettuce.

She pushed a napkin across the table and said, "Can I have your autograph, too?" He laughed, and she thought, *Yeah, I can be funny. I can make him laugh. Maybe I have something besides an inordinate amount of salad knowl-edge that I can bring to the relationship.* It was maybe the most perfect moment of her life, and as if to tempt fate, she thought, *Someone should take a picture.*

The shouts came first. "Lance! Lance! Lance, look over here."

And then she saw it—the bright light—the *you've almost reached the end of the tunnel* light that burned from the corner of her eyes like a television that's about to die, little pieces of static that swirled and blurred until there was nothing left of her vision but a field of pure white snow.

"Lance, how about a wave?" someone yelled. "Lance! Lance!"

Julia threw her hand to her face and tried to shield her eyes from the glare, but the lights flashed hot and bright again, burning through the night. She felt a hand on her wrist, felt Lance's arm was around her shoulders. She buried her head against his chest.

"Lance!" they yelled again from behind her. "Lance!"

"Get him in the car!" someone shouted, and Julia looked up to see Wes strolling toward them. She didn't know if he was following them, or psychic, or if he just had the greatest response time in the world. She didn't care. She just knew that she was being pushed through the kitchen—past steaming pots and rows of men speaking in Spanish, and the only words she understood were "Lance Collins."

Someone pushed open a door, and soon Julia was being dragged into a huge, black SUV.

Breathless and silent, they sat side by side for a long time. The SUV swerved violently, veering into traffic, and Julia felt herself fall into Lance as they turned. He wrapped an arm around her, holding her there. Her hand rested on his chest, and she felt his breathing slow.

Lance turned and looked through the tinted window. The city lights blurred and flashed outside as they climbed into the hills.

"So, typical first date?" she asked, needing to hear him laugh.

"No." He turned to face her. "It was better."

Chapter Seventeen

> You cannot hope to pick up from the deck a card which is no longer there.

From: James Family Farm

To: OK Lady

Subject: Quite a nice picture in today's paper

Someone we know made the paper today. It's a really nice picture. You look thin. Are you eating enough?

Would you like me to send you some meat?

Love,

Mom

"Julia," she heard Lance whisper. "Julia." He shook her slightly, pulling her from a dream so that when she opened her eyes and saw him sitting on the corner of the bed, she wondered for a second where reality began and ended.

Then, her hand brushed against the denim of his jeans. She saw the bag on the floor at his feet.

"No." He eased her back down on the pillow. "Don't get up."

"What time—"

"It's early."

And it must have been. There wasn't any light—not even stars or the residual glare of the city that rested at the bottom of the hills, so she just stared at him through the eerie, green glow of the clock she didn't look at and said, "You're leaving." It wasn't a question. It was an inevitability.

"Yeah. Wes just called. There are some—"

"It's the middle of the night," she said, shifting on the bed, trying to remember if this was part of the dream she'd been having, trying to know what she was supposed to say.

"Not in New York."

She started to protest, to ask questions, to do the math in her foggy head and somehow tell him that he had time—that they'd talk about it in the morning. But then Lance placed one arm on either side of her and leaned down to kiss her good-bye.

"Where will you go from there?" she asked because she knew that wasn't just it. It wasn't just a quick flight to New York and a fast flight home. The bag at his feet was too heavy. His hands held too tightly to her shoulders for that to be it.

"I'll be back in a few days."

"Oh," Julia said.

"Don't leave," he said as if she might bolt from the bed and flee just that second, as if there was already a car idling outside. "I want you to stay, Julia. I want Nina to decorate. I want you to write or swim or shop or just . . . I'm gonna be back. I really want . . . I really need you to be here. Stay a few days," he said in a way that was part reminder; part question.

"Okay," Julia said.

And then he picked up his bag and walked toward the door. He stopped, though, one last time and looked at her. "Go back to sleep. I'm sorry I woke you."

"I'm not."

The security system beeped a few minutes later as Lance disarmed and rearmed the alarm, but she sensed more than heard him leave.

"So," Caroline said the next morning, "how was it?"

How was what? Julia wanted to ask but didn't. She was afraid to speak. She was afraid her sister would figure out that it was eleven-thirty in the morning and Julia was still in bed. Farmgirls have been disinherited for less.

"The date!" Caroline screamed, desperate for details. She wanted a story about flowers and five-star restaurants and dancing under the stars, but she would have settled for anything more cultured than the Cartoon Network and Pizza Hut two-for-one specials.

Caroline didn't get out much.

Julia eased upright and squinted against the sun. Her voice was groggy as she said, "It was fine."

"ARE YOU STILL IN BED?" Caroline shouted, and Julia remembered that her sister's talents were wasted as a stay-at-home mom. Caroline belonged in the CIA.

"Don't tell Mom!" Julia blurted then untangled herself from the sheets and swung her feet to the floor. She felt her hair sticking out from odd angles, then she remembered Lance leaving in the middle of the night. She recalled the paparazzi flashes and being shoved into an SUV. She remembered how things can go from perfect to terrifying in a flash—literally. She remembered what she had slept so long to forget.

"It was a long night, Caroline."

"Why? What happened? Was it not wonderful?"

There wasn't a simple answer, *but is there ever?* Julia wondered. Julia knew she couldn't tell Caroline that the date had been covered by paparazzi, that Wes had driven them home as if they were in the seventh grade in the back of her dad's car, that so far nothing in California seemed to fit— except at the hip strip.

"I bet it was wonderful," Caroline said again, and Julia knew there were things Caroline didn't want to hear, and for the most part they were the things Julia didn't want to say. Julia was alone again, this time in a different way. She woke up in a castle, but Prince Charming was gone. How was she supposed to tell her sister that? Some people never stop believing in fairy tales.

"Joan Rivers sat at the next table," Julia said, amazed by how easily the lie had come. "She complimented me on my outfit."

When Caroline didn't squeal or scream or ask a million questions, Julia worried that she might have gone too far. Joan Rivers at the next table—believable. A compliment—too much. But Caroline needed the fantasy. Julia heard her sigh.

"What was *she* wearing?" Caroline asked, and Julia told her, "Black pantsuit. Lots of gold necklaces and a mink coat."

The lies were even easier now and Julia almost believed them. She could see Joan Rivers then, her blond hair perfectly teased and sprayed, looking more than a little like Felicia Wallace, and Julia wondered if that connection had been pinballing around in her subconscious all the time, waiting to get out.

"Mink?" Caroline asked. "Isn't that a little un-P.C.?"

"She's Joan Rivers. You think she cares?"

And Julia felt a little guilty, making her pretend-friend Joan come off so bad, but Caroline didn't care, and somehow Julia thought the real Joan wouldn't mind either. The real Joan would get off on the charade.

"She's totally skinnier than she looks on TV," Julia added for good measure.

From fifteen hundred miles away she heard her sister's jealous sigh.

♥

"Helloooooooo!"

Julia found Nina and Amanda downstairs, looking through the French doors as the old woman floated toward the house. Nina said, "I don't know why we have to open the door for her. She could just scream and break the glass and come on in."

"Let's leave that for emergencies, okay?" Julia said just as Sybil cried, "Hello, helloooooo!"

Sybil was in her usual dressing gown again that morning, but instead of letting her white hair blow wild, she'd wrapped her head in red silk and secured it with a silver broach. She was ready for her close-up in true *Sunset Boulevard* form. She was old Hollywood—emphasis on the old.

"Hello, Sybil," Julia said, welcoming her inside. "Don't you look nice?"

"Oh, dear, that's so sweet of you." She placed one hand

on either side of Julia's—a handshake sandwich, but her skin felt thin, papery. Julia wondered if Sybil was getting enough to eat.

She seemed fragile and weak, right up until the point when she turned to Julia and asked, "Is it true that there are goats that faint when they hear a scream?"

Julia nearly spit out a mouthful of the pulp-free orange juice that there always seemed to be gallons of in the refrigerator. She studied Sybil, saw how serious the woman was, and wondered which was worse, that she *looked* like someone who would know the answer to that question, or that she *was* someone who would know the answer to that question.

"Yes." Julia nodded, decided there were worse things to be than *resident goat expert*, and took another swig of juice. "Actually, it's a defense mechanism. They play dead—like an opossum."

"Ooh!" Sybil said, folding her hands together. She bounced up and down slightly. Her eyes glowed. "I must admit I've been a while between roles now, and I thought that they might help me to stay in practice . . . you know . . . with my screaming."

Julia and Nina gave each other a nod, and Nina said, "Oh, I think that's a great idea. You should *totally* get one."

Sadly, Julia knew that Nina wasn't being facetious or sarcastic—Nina just wanted a neighborhood goat.

Sybil crossed her arms and drummed her red fingernails against her sleeve, pondering this. "Yes, I may have to invest in a goat. A fainting goat."

Julia studied the old woman. Her eyes were shining like her rhinestone broach. Goats—goats were the key to her big comeback. She was on her way.

Then Julia looked at Sybil's frail fingers, her thin arms, and she remembered how easy it is to skip meals when you're the only one eating. "Sybil, would you like to stay and have some lunch with us?" she asked, but the woman waved her away.

"Oh no, no. That's very sweet, but I can't impose. I just wanted to ask about the goat and . . ." She trailed off and looked around.

"Yes?" Julia prompted.

A slight blush spread onto Sybil's sunken cheeks. "Well," she said, "I have a little favor to ask of the man of the house."

Julia listened to the empty rooms, the hollow echo she'd known so well for so long, and said, "That would be me," and for so much of her life—it had been.

"Watch your step, dear," Sybil said, but Julia knew the only thing she was at risk of tripping over was her jaw. Where Lance's house was empty and sprawling, Sybil's was quaint and full. Every wall held a photo, every shelf a memento. A grand piano sat in a bay window with a shawl thrown over its glossy surface, and a dozen silver frames showed black-and-white images of the same flawless, utterly stunning face.

"Sybil!" Julia exclaimed, reaching for one. "You were beautiful!"

Then, she realized how insulted the woman should have been—that sometimes *were* is a terrible, terrible verb.

But the old woman didn't hear her, or if she did, she didn't care. She just came to stand beside Julia and lifted one of the framed images from its place of honor. A wrinkled face filled the glass, an overlay over the smooth perfect skin of the picture, and Julia wondered if Sybil thought it was a mirror instead of a looking glass to the past.

"It's a stunning picture," Julia said, trying to keep things as firmly in the present tense as possible, but Sybil only sighed.

"Yes, well," Sybil started, "I suppose they'll do." Then she returned the frame to the piano and turned from the images as if she was afraid of looking too hard. "I haven't had new head shots taken in ages. Perhaps it's time to do that."

But Julia couldn't think of a thing to say. She fingered the shawl. It felt silky beneath her fingers—not like something an interior decorator had brought, but rather like something Sybil had worn. Standing close to it, Julia thought she smelled rum and fresh gardenias. She looked at Sybil and somehow knew—really knew—that in her day, the woman had really known how to dance.

"We filmed *Zombie Holiday* in Cuba, you know?" Sybil said as if reading Julia's mind. "I do love Cuba." Light fell through the leaded glass windows and danced in her eyes. "I should insist we film my next project there." She glanced down at the photographs but her stare didn't linger long. "Yes. I'll certainly insist we film in Cuba."

And then Sybil beamed. She was going to get headshots taken. She was going to buy a goat and go to Cuba. She was going to stage a comeback—if one was really needed in Sybil's mind, in Sybil's world.

Julia glanced at the movie posters on the walls and quickly calculated that Sybil's prime had lasted seven years— between *The Mummy's Bride* and *Monsters at Midnight*. Seven years.

Julia's had lasted six.

"Sybil," Julia said when the silence was finally too much, too sad. "Was there something I could help you with?"

"Oh," Sybil said with a start. "Yes, dear. A lightbulb. I fell changing one last year and my doctor made me promise not to try again." Then Sybil whispered, "I'm fairly sure the studio put him up to it—I think it's in my contract."

"Yes," Julia said. "Of course."

As Sybil turned and started down the hall, her footsteps

barely made a sound on the tile floors as if she were a burglar in her own home, stealing something from the woman who used to live there.

♠

When she got back to the house, Julia wasted no time in finding Nina.

"Lance wants you to decorate," she said. "He wants us to stay. He wants . . ." She trailed off, thinking for a moment about Sybil's cluttered house and empty life, her aching need to hang on to a spotlight long since dim, and Julia turned it over in her mind one more time—the nagging question of which is better, to never know a glory day or to live your life riding on fame's anticlimactic wake. "So just . . . do your thing."

"Really? Really! The whole nine yards, the kit and caboodle, the whole shebang, the—"

"Yeah, Nina." Julia drew a breath and looked around the empty rooms. "Yeah," she said again.

Chapter Eighteen

Be prepared to lose some hands—even seasoned experts can't always go gin. Losing a hand doesn't necessarily mean you'll lose the game.

From: James Family Farm

TO: OK Lady

Subject: Another pretty day here

It's another pretty day here. Dad and I went by and looked at your house, Julia. It's looking quite nice.

I took Sam cinnamon rolls and he asked about you.

When are you coming home?

Love,

Mom

Okay," Nina said bright and early the next morning. "Are we clear on everything?"

"Yes," Julia said, rolling her eyes. She gripped Nina's careful list and read her instructions for the day,

"Nine o'clock, painters arrive to work on dining room—make them do the trim first. If they don't want to do the trim first, call 911." She glanced up at Nina. "Yeah, I'll probably just call you instead, if that's okay."

"Fine," Nina said. "Whatever. Just don't let them start on the walls without talking to me."

She scanned through the rest of her assignments—the jobs and tasks and purposes of a woman who is nesting. Her day was full of furniture that needed delivering and draperies that needed measuring, and art that needed hanging. Her day was full.

She looked down at the list in her hands as, in her peripheral vision, Nina gathered her purse and checked her notebook. "Hey, Nina, I had an e-mail from Mom. She and Dad went to look at the house," she said then felt the need to clarify. "My house?"

My house. The words sounded strange, foreign, yet vaguely remembered like a song she hadn't sung in a long time. A game she'd forgotten how to play.

"Yeah," Nina said, sounding distracted. "I talked to Sam yesterday. Roof's on. Carpet's going in."

"Oh," Julia said. "Then it's just as well I'm not there—right? They can't do that with people in the house?"

Nina was digging in her purse, her hair falling over her eyes. "Have you seen my cell?"

"What?" Julia asked as Nina walked into the kitchen and

grabbed the cordless phone, dialed a number, and held her purse to her ear until it started ringing.

"Okay!" Nina said brightly, heading for the door. "I've got everything. Now, are you going to be okay being in charge while I'm gone? I know this isn't really your comfort zone." She held her hands up, marking the words with imaginary quotation marks, mocking Julia in her special, Nina-like way. "Amanda's here if you—"

"Nina," Julia said. "Just go."

By one, Julia was tired of biting back the phrase *Don't ask me*, exhausted from offering opinions, making decisions. She'd never known how much energy it takes to care what color the curtains are.

When the phone rang, Amanda answered, "L.C. Enterprises," repeating the name of Lance's newly minted limited liability corporation. "I'm afraid Mr. Collins is unavailable. I'd be happy to take a message," the young girl said professionally, as Julia wondered whether that would always be the answer even if Lance was standing right beside her, even if it was Julia on the other end of the line. But then Amanda exclaimed, "Oh! Wow! It's so nice to meet you. Sure, we'll be here," and without another word, she disconnected and trotted toward the kitchen.

"Amanda!" Julia yelled, following her through the rooms. "Who was that?"

Amanda was already cradling a cluster of grapes in her cupped hand and was holding one between the front of her teeth as she stared at Julia. "Lance's mom," she said simply, and Julia froze. "She's going to be in town and asked if she could drop some stuff off, so I said sure." She was chewing the fruit, putting another piece in her mouth before she noticed Julia's dazed expression. "That is cool? Isn't it? I mean, she's his *mom*."

There are certain things a woman likes to do before meeting the mother her boyfriend idolizes . . . little things like wash your hair and bake banana bread.

"Amanda, listen to me," Julia said as she slapped her hands together once and hard, trying to harness the girl's attention to that particular place and time. "When is she coming?"

"Oh," Amanda said, rolling her eyes. "See, she is passing through going to San Diego but the car was low on oil and one of the boxes was—"

"Amanda." Julia couldn't believe what she was saying. "Long-story-short."

"Right now."

♥

Okay, Julia thought as she looked in the mirror, staring at her "game face." *What do I know?* she asked herself. *She likes Lance. I like Lance. She likes theater. I was in my high school production of* Our Town. *She's . . .*

At the front door.

A buzzer sounded throughout the house and she heard Amanda's muffled, "I'll get it."

The woman in the mirror, however, didn't budge. Of all the times Julia had imagined meeting the woman who had raised Lance almost single-handedly, she had thought he'd be beside her, beaming at them both, his hand in hers as he looked at his mother and said, *Mom, this is Julia.* Robert Wells might have had an Oscar and a star-studded career that spanned three decades, but Lance's mother had something his father would probably never have—Lance. He was supposed to be her guide on this oh-so-intimidating foray into *girlfriendom*, but instead Lance was in another world, and Julia knew this was one journey she'd be making alone.

"I love Lance. She loves Lance," Julia said to herself as if courage was an emotion that can be pumped into a body like helium into a balloon, and with that, she floated toward the door.

Donna Collins was in the foyer when Julia appeared at the top of the stairs. Even from that angle, Julia could see where Lance got his good metabolism. The woman was tall and straight with honey blond and slightly frizzy hair pulled into a ponytail at the base of her neck and secured with a strap of leather. She looked as out-of-place among the chaos as Julia felt, and for a second, Julia thought she might have found an ally, someone with a voice loud enough and strong enough to call out and tell everyone in the room to stop. Someone like Julia used to be.

But then, the woman looked up.

"Oh," she said coolly. "Hello."

Julia had wanted to stand there and quietly study her like scientists observe animals, trying to understanding them by the way they pace the walls of their cages; she had wanted to know, to understand, to maybe pick up a trick or two about being someone Lance adores, but the woman stepped closer, and Julia knew she hadn't come to give pointers.

The smell of paint wafted through the house, giving everyone a high—giving Julia a headache—and Donna had to twice step aside for the workmen to pass as they carried their tools in and out.

Julia forced her best smile. "Hi . . ." Julia started then trailed off. *Donna?* she tried. *Ms. Collins? Mrs. Wells? Mom?* "Hi! It's really nice to meet you. I'm Julia. Lance has told me so much . . ." she said, starting to rush forward but stopping suddenly as she realized she didn't know what to do when she reached her. *Do we shake hands? Do we hug? Oh, God, please tell me we're not going to have to hug.*

"Hello." Donna Collins's voice was even, measured. A

team of men came through the front door then, carrying an antique armoire.

"Where you want this, lady?" one of the men asked, and without thinking, Julia said, "In the entertainment room." She gestured to a set of pocket doors.

An odd look lighted on Donna's face, not settling really, just passing over like the shadow of a cloud, and Julia didn't know what it meant—she just knew it wasn't good.

"Sorry about that," she said. "It's crazy around here today. If we'd known you were coming—oh—not that it's your fault. You're always welcome to come by. Our home is—Oh, not that *I* live here. I don't . . . live here, I mean. Nina and I are just . . . well . . . Lance asked me to help him . . ."

Finally Julia saw Amanda standing behind Donna's shoulder, slowly dragging one long, manicured hand across her throat, and Julia blurted, "He's not here!"

And then Donna Collins looked her up and down and said, "You're a writer?" Not: *You're a writer* exclamation point, or even: *You're a writer* period. It was definitely: *You're a writer* question mark, also known as "Would you look at what has become of the literary arts in this country?"

"Lady?" another deliveryman said. This time he held one end of an enormous headboard to a four-poster bed.

"Top of the stairs," Julia said. "I'm sorry. It's. . . . Like I said. It's a crazy day."

"Yes," Donna said. "I can see that. I just have had some of Lance's things in storage, and since I was driving through . . . Well . . . I'll put these wherever you want them." She gestured to the boxes and bags that filled her arms and lay piled on the floor as if to identify *these*.

Julia was quick to react. "Oh, no. Let—"

"Are you going to have the maid do it?" the woman snapped.

Maid? Julia wondered then realized. "Amanda?" She laughed. "Oh, she's not a maid. She's Lance's personal assistant."

"I thought Lance was out of town."

"Oh, he is. But Amanda is his local assistant. She doesn't travel with him." She smiled, tried to brush off the misunderstanding, but "personal assistant" wasn't exactly helping her case, because the woman seemed to grow even harder.

Julia grabbed one of the black plastic sacks and shuffled the box to her hip. Before Lance's mom could say a word, she blurted, "Let's take these upstairs."

They each took an armload and started up the stairs. Away from Amanda and the workers and the bright light of the foyer windows, Julia felt the weight settle back down upon her. She stole a glance at the woman behind her and thought, *This is Lance's mom.*

"It's certainly . . ." She heard the woman struggle for words. "Large."

"Oh," Julia said. "Would you like a tour, or—"

"No," Lance's mother stated flatly. "No thank you. I think I've seen enough."

As they placed the boxes and bags in a huge empty closet, Julia heard Amanda yell, "Julia! The painters are working on the walls!"

"Oh jeez!" Julia said, remembering the wrath of Nina if anything happened to those walls. "They're not supposed to . . ." She trailed off when she read Donna's expression. ". . . do that. Um, could you wait just one . . ." She held up a finger, begging the woman's patience, but Lance's mother was already halfway down the stairs.

"Wait, please," Julia said, rushing to the foyer. "I know it's a little—"

"Lady," one of the deliverymen called to her, "you got someplace specific you want this plasma TV or are we just supposed to guess?"

"I'll be right there," Julia called behind her. "Really, Mrs. . . . I mean, Ms. . . . I mean . . . Donn—" She took a deep breath. "Would you like to stay for lunch or—"

"No." Donna Collins shook her head sharply and eased toward the door. "No, I think I should be leaving."

A loud crash echoed through the house and Julia prayed that wasn't what plasma TVs sounded like when they fell and broke into a million pieces. Still, she managed to keep her gaze firmly on Lance's mother as she said, "It was so nice meeting you. When Lance gets home, we'll have to—"

Another crash and the overwhelming stench of wet paint made Julia jump again.

"I really should be going." Donna Collins reached down to open the door. "I'm very sorry I missed seeing Lance."

The door closed, and Julia stood looking at it for a long time. "I'm sorry you missed seeing him, too."

Chapter Nineteen

The glory of gin is that it's a game that can be played almost anywhere. But depending on the conditions, one player may have a home court advantage.

Julia wasn't really sure what she was doing until after she'd already called the cab company and given them the address. She didn't leave a note. She probably wouldn't have remembered her purse if it hadn't been sitting by the phone, staring at her.

She started walking, pausing only once, at the door, to hear Amanda say, probably on a cell phone, probably to Nina, "It looks ivory to me. Isn't it supposed to be eggshell?" Then Julia reached for the door, needing the cool wind and the warm sun and to be miles and miles away from that place where the world stopped to differentiate between shades of white.

She reached the gates and saw the cab on the horizon, so she sank to the curb and waited.

"Where to?" the driver asked, but Julia didn't have a reply. "Airport?" the man guessed. "Mercedes dealership? Plastic surgeon?"

"No," Julia said, shaking her head and trying to clear the cobwebs from her mind. "Can we just drive? Can you do that—just drive around or something?"

"You want to see the sights?" the man asked.

"Yeah. Sure. Let's see the sights."

He turned around and said, "Okay."

By the time they reached Sunset Boulevard, Julia had learned that her driver's name was Pedro, he was taking night classes at a local junior college, and he was going to make famous documentaries about Hispanic culture.

"So what about you?" he asked. "Why doesn't your boyfriend show you the sights?"

"Oh," Julia said. She wiped her eyes but there weren't any tears. She wondered for a second what that said about her, but then she realized it couldn't say anything good, so she just turned to stare out the window. "He's busy," she told the driver.

"Movie star?" Pedro guessed.

"Movie star," Julia answered, but Pedro didn't ask which one. Instead, he nodded slowly as if he picked movie stars' girlfriends up off curbs every day—and evidently took them to the airport, the Mercedes dealership, or the plastic surgeon.

Two hours later they went through a drive-thru and Julia bought them both burgers and chocolate shakes. They sat on the hood of the car and watched the ocean while they ate. An hour after that, Pedro made Julia buy a disposable camera, and he took her picture with her hands pressed into the palm prints of Rita Hayworth. They were a perfect fit.

When a family of tourists insisted on taking a picture of Pedro and Julia together, he put his arm around her and smiled and told her later that she should hang on to this picture because it might be worth a lot of money when his documentary gets made. Somehow, she believed him.

At five-thirty he told her that his daughter had a dance recital at seven and he needed to go home first to change and get his film equipment.

"Oh," Julia said, feeling like they were back at the airport–Mercedes dealership–plastic surgeon portion of the day—like those were the three prizes she could choose from.

"I don't have to take you home," Pedro said softly. He looked at her in the rearview mirror—really seeing her. "There's a coffee shop not far from where I picked you up. What about I take you there?"

"Okay," Julia said.

"And if you're still there at ten o'clock, you can call and I'll come take you home."

"Okay."

"It's okay," Pedro said reassuringly. "You'll be okay."

◆

The coffee shop was called the Fade Inn and they served veggie wraps and green tea and about thirty different kinds of coffee. The sign above the cash register said that they had free wireless Internet for customers and Julia had never seen so many laptop computers and notecards and books featuring the word *Screenwriting* in her life.

But even though it was a public venue, she knew it was private, too. The people there were regulars. She'd walked into their office. They typed and stretched and sipped their caffeine because they were probably too squeamish to have it hooked directly into an IV, and they looked at her as if she were the competition. Even without the books and the laptops and the red pens stuck behind their ears, she would have known she was among writers. There was a primitive instinct, an animal smell that told her she was among her own kind.

Julia found a table and ordered something, not really so much to eat as to have an excuse to sit there, soaking in it, getting a hit off other people's creativity.

A blue Macintosh glowed like neon in the dark corner. The guy behind it would talk to himself for awhile, then type awhile, then hold the DELETE key down and wipe away thirty minutes' worth of work in one fell swoop. Then he'd close his eyes for a minute and start it all again.

When the waitress came to refill Julia's iced tea, she whispered, "Is he watching me now?"

"Who?" Julia whispered.

"Stalker guy," the waitress said, jerking her head toward a man on the far side of the room who spent one minute looking at his screen for every five minutes he spent looking at the waitress.

Julia looked behind her. He didn't even bother to glance away. "Yeah."

"Crap," she said and walked away. Five minutes later, she folded up her apron and left. Two minutes after that, he followed. Three minutes later, the girl slipped in through the back and went back to work.

"There you are!" Nina yelled when Julia walked through the door at half past ten. "Where have you been? Did you know we've been worried sick?" Nina went on and on, but Julia just walked toward the stairs. She wanted to go to bed. She wanted to sleep. She wanted to do anything but stand there listening to Nina's cries of ". . . Lance's mother . . ." and ". . . Amanda called . . ." and ". . . ransom note . . ."

"I'm sorry, Neen," Julia whispered, and she was, but the roller coaster of the day had left her too numb to say so.

She tried to push by but Nina grabbed her shoulders, proving two things. One, her best friend really did love her. And two, Nina was deceptively strong. Nina dragged her toward the kitchen and pushed her into a chair. Amanda had appeared by that time, and Julia saw how pale the two of them were.

"Julia," Nina said, shaking her, "what happened?"

"I think . . ." Julia started. "I think maybe it's time I go home."

When she was in school, boys used to tell her she was the kind of girl they'd love to take home to meet their mother— she was the kind of girl they wanted to marry. Of course, they told her this while they were dating other girls—the dating girls—the fun girls. But now the dating girls all seemed to have become something else—wives. And Julia, it turned out, wasn't good at meeting mothers.

Nothing, she decided, is ever as it seems.

"Julia," Nina said, "you've got to—"

"What?" Julia threw her hands to her sides, vulnerable, prone. "What? Tell me, because I don't know. I don't know how to meet the mother. I don't know how to set up the house. I don't know how to be the girlfriend. I just don't know. I just don't. I just don't know!"

She started to get up. She wanted to crawl into bed and sleep a thousand years. "I—"

"Julia," Nina yelled, "JASON'S MOTHER LOVED ME!"

Julia felt something boiling inside her. "Thanks for pointing that out, Neen," she spat. "That really—"

"And look how we turned out."

Chapter Twenty

The winning player doesn't have to go gin. Usually, the game is won by the person who knocks as quickly as possible.

From: James Family Farm

To: OK Lady

Subject: Message from Sam

Sam called to say the carpet is in. It looks quite nice—very luxurious.

Don't tell Daddy what you paid for it.

Love,

Mom

"Hi. Welcome back," the waitress said as she stood over Julia, a plastic menu in each hand. "Can I give you some advice?"

Julia looked around the room then said, "Sure."

"Don't sit there. Duncan sits there. I mean, it's not his seat officially or anything, it's just that people get used to having certain seats."

"Like church?"

"Sure, yeah, I guess."

"Okay." Julia gathered her things. "Is there someplace that someone doesn't usually sit?"

She followed the waitress to a table in the back, then something occurred to Julia. "Hey, isn't this where Stalker Guy was sitting last night?"

A guilty smile flashed over the young woman's face. "Yeah," she said. "Maybe if someone takes his seat, he'll leave."

"You think that will work?" Julia asked.

The waitress shrugged. "Worth a shot."

Halfway through the day, Julia decided it was very much like church. No one spoke, but people said a lot of prayers—she could tell by the way they typed and read and held their hands clasped behind their heads and stretched. They were praying for agents and publicists and six-figure deals. They were praying for what she had.

"What are you working on?" the waitress said and Julia jumped.

It took a moment for her heart to slow down before she stretched and said, "I don't know."

"You're a writer, though, right?"

Julia looked at her blank screen, her scattered, senseless notes and muttered, "I used to be."

The waitress shrugged and slid into the seat across from Julia's. She nodded as if this wasn't big news, as if people laid sad and profound declarations on her doorstep every day, and maybe they did because she cocked her head and said, "I used to be a shrink."

Julia must have looked as shocked as she felt because the waitress nodded and smiled. "Oh yeah. Stanford med school. Leather couches. The whole two-hundred-dollar-an-hour package. But then I woke up one day and decided I wanted to write a screenplay, so I started coming here. Six months later I realized I didn't really want to write a screenplay—I just didn't want to be a shrink anymore."

"Wow," Julia said.

"Yeah," said the waitress. "Talk about plot points." Then she got up and went to refill someone's coffee, and Julia was left to wonder how many people are one thing simply because they don't want to be something else.

"Hey," Lance called to the driver. "Stop the car."

As the town car pulled to the side of the street, Lance looked behind him at the burgundy awning that stretched from Stella's restaurant to the street—the place where he'd first stood with Julia, waiting out the rain.

He walked down the sidewalk toward the place for no

real reason other than a strange magnetic pull. That was where it all had started. He felt like he was returning to a place of his childhood—like an old house or kindergarten hall. He had to see if everything looked smaller.

What if my agent and her agent hadn't picked that same restaurant to eat at on the same day? What if there had been two cabs instead of one? What if it hadn't been raining?

The lights were off, and a sign hung in the window, saying, AFTER THIRTY-FIVE YEARS IN BUSINESS, WE ARE REGRETFULLY CLOSING OUR DOORS.

He pulled out his phone and dialed.

"Hello," Julia said, her voice as clear through the line as if she were still standing beside him, looking out at the passing traffic and storefronts along the street.

"Hey," he said.

"Hey yourself," she said, but he didn't say anything; he just kept staring at the sign, remembering how Julia had loved that little out-of-the-way place—how she had been coming for years, long before he sat down at her table.

She sighed. He wanted to hold her hand. "So, where are you?" she asked, and he read the sign again, trying to find a loophole in the truth.

"Stella's."

"Ooh, don't tell me that," she complained. "I'm so jealous. I love their eggplant Parmesan. Is Giovanni working?"

"No," Lance said, looking at the dark room behind the dusty glass where men in long white aprons used to float between the tables carrying steaming baskets of bread. "I don't think he's here."

"Well, that's too bad. I would have had you say hi to him for me. You know, I've known him for years."

"I know," Lance said.

"Oh, I miss Stella's."

He looked at the dark empty space. "And it misses you, too."

♥

When the message came, Julia didn't read it. Not until after she'd changed her clothes and pulled her hair back and washed the faint coffee smell of the Fade Inn from her hands. Not until she'd told Nina and Amanda that she was going to work upstairs for a while—that she was on a deadline, that she wasn't to be disturbed. Not until she'd crossed her legs as if to meditate and centered the laptop on her thighs. It was waiting there for her, she knew, but the longer she could delay in opening it, the longer it would be until she would know something was wrong, that Harvey suspected what she knew.

From: Harvey

To: OK Lady

Subject: How's it going, kiddo?

Hi sweetheart. Hope everything is going well in California. Let me know when you have something you want me to look at.

   Or if you want to talk.

Love ya, kiddo,

Harvey

She read it once, then twice, then again for good measure. Then she glanced at the phone and felt her fingers tick, dialing out the number as they rested in her lap.

It would be so simple.

It would be so hard.

She felt guilty just for thinking of the message she wanted to send, for wishing she could go back to the ten seconds in Lance's foyer when Amanda thought Nina was the girlfriend, the author, the things Julia no longer knew how to be.

She thought about Harvey and her parents. And Lance. Suddenly her life was full of people she didn't deserve—love she'd never earned. She wondered what it would feel like to hit REPLY and spill out all the things she couldn't say, all the truths that she held and served in small, measured, unlethal doses. All she had to do was REPLY write two final words: *I quit.*

From: OK Lady

To: Harvey

Subject: checking in

Hi Harvey! Greetings from sunny California. Hope you're still feeling well. Things are great here. I'm finding lots of time for writing. No problems.

Take care,

Julia

Julia read the message. Then reread it. She clicked SEND, knowing she might have a knack for fiction after all, as downstairs Amanda sang, "Julia, I think you have a visitor."

◆

"Caroline!" Julia cried out—but it wasn't an *oh-I've-missed-you-and-I-have-to-hug-you* cry. It was a *what-in-the-world-are-you-doing* cry. Her sister knew the difference.

"I can explain!"

"Caroline!" Julia yelled again, stepping closer, her mind racing as the questions started to flow. "Are Mom and Dad all right . . . where are Steve and the kids . . . are the kids all right . . . how did you get here . . . what are you doing?"

Through all that, Caroline was mute. She was wearing big sunglasses and a wide-brimmed floppy hat, and she stood in the sunshine smiling the smile of someone who is a thousand miles away from responsibility of any kind. The smile of relief.

"Caroline," Julia said again as she reached the door, "*what* are you doing here?"

But instead of answering, Caroline just yelled, "Surprise!"

"Yes," Julia said, "it is."

"Hi, I'm Amanda," Amanda said. "I've heard so much about you. It's so great to meet you. I have a sister, and we're super close, except for this one time when we were like seventeen and . . . well . . . long-story-short . . . eyelash curlers."

Amanda sighed as Caroline stepped forward and cried, "Me, too!" And then they hugged as if relieved to finally find someone who understood. They both spoke the language of the professionally put-upon, and now they were soul mates, kindred spirits, best-friends-forever. Just like that, Julia knew that Caroline might never leave.

Then Julia glanced down and noticed that a small hard-sided suitcase sat at her sister's feet, wrapped in duct tape and covered with a thin layer of frost.

"Um, Caroline . . ." Julia pointed to the bag. "Your clothes are frosting over."

"*Oh.* That bag isn't for clothes," Caroline said in a don't-be-silly manner. "It's for meat."

She picked it up and started into the house, not pausing to look at the rooms or comment on the view. It was as if she had been there a thousand times before and was just drop-ping by. "Mom and Dad insisted I bring you some steaks and stuff. I think they're terrified you're gonna starve to death."

When she reached the kitchen, she put the suitcase on the counter, opened it and then the freezer portion of the big Subzero, and went to work. All Julia could do was stare at her—her sister with her "slept funny on the plane" hair and arms full of frozen pot roasts. Her sister who was a thou-sand miles from where she was supposed to be.

"Okay," Julia snapped, finally broken by the silence. "You're seriously freaking me out." But Caroline didn't say anything, and the only sound was the steady hum of the freezer as she arranged and rearranged the frost-covered packages as if they were a puzzle she had to get right.

"Caroline," Julia said softly, somehow knowing not to shout. "Caroline, what are you doing here?"

But her sister smiled and half faced her, still absorbed in her task. "I came to see you, silly."

"But Caroline, what about Steve? The kids?"

Caroline slid aside a flank steak and made room for a roast. Julia was almost sure she hadn't heard until Caroline said calmly, "Steve has decided to take a leave-of-absence from the firm." She didn't turn around, and the words were chilly as they reached Julia's ears.

"Can he do that?" Julia asked.

Caroline shrugged. "I guess so. They got sued last year by a woman who was denied maternity leave—can you imagine that? In this day and age a woman getting denied maternity leave—by a *law firm*?" She waved it off then, as if the woman was lucky she didn't have to stay home and change diapers for three months. As if Caroline knew better. "So now he's taking paternity leave, he calls it. Like Nick isn't crawling already. But he's taking paternity leave so that he can have a"—she paused and made imaginary quotation marks above her head—*"more active role in the kids' lives."*

"Okay," Julia said calmly. "So what are *you* doing?"

Caroline slammed the freezer door, and even from ten feet away, Julia felt the rush of frozen air when her sister said, "I'm letting him."

Julia couldn't sleep that night, and she realized that her insomnia had been creeping back slowly, sneaking in like a thief in the night, stealing a few minutes here and there until all she could do was stare at the ceiling and long for a game of solitaire.

For a second she thought about calling Lance, but it was late in California, no doubt later wherever he was, but where that was exactly, she didn't know. Amanda had no doubt told her. There was probably a note hanging on the fridge.

She laughed. *The fridge.* Caroline had flown fifteen hundred miles to get away from stuff like that, but notes on refrigerators were universal, she guessed, no matter how much the kitchens cost.

Her bedroom was weird—too hot under the covers. Too cold out of them. She finally kicked one leg on top so that half of her was freezing and half was sweating, thinking she'd be just right in the middle. But it didn't work.

At four o'clock she gave up and went downstairs. She crept into the entertainment room, slid the pocket doors closed behind her, sank onto the plush new sofa, and turned on the TV.

A pink-clad spokeswoman told her about a knife set that could revolutionize her world if she ordered right away. An evangelist offered salvation with a 1-800 number. There were a hundred ways to change her life at that hour, and all of them just a phone call away, but the phones were in the other room, Julia realized. Her life wasn't going to be changing after all.

She moved through the channels, lulled and dizzy with the quick flashes of light in the dark room; she squinted; it made her head hurt, but she couldn't stop. When she saw his face, she thought she'd drifted to sleep, that she was dreaming. But then she clicked back quickly, and knew that she'd been half-right. It wasn't Lance. But it was close.

Robert Wells had been two years older than Lance was when he won his Academy Award. That night, Julia lay on the couch and almost forgot who she was watching. Lance had his father's eyes, his smile, his talent. And when she closed her eyes, she heard his voice, and finally drifted off to sleep.

Chapter Twenty-one

It's important to remember that in Hollywood gin, scores are cumulative.

From: James Family Farm

To: OK Lady

Subject: Just checking on you

Nothing new here today. Daddy kind of hurt his leg, but the vet was here and said it was nothing, so he's not going to the doctor.

We're so lucky to have such a good vet nearby.

Love,

Mom

Oh, have mercy, Julia thought, channeling Nina, as she stood in the doorway and watched the sun stream around the figure of the man who had come calling. He wore faded jeans and a button-down shirt and looked as ordinary—and as extraordinary—as a man could possibly be.

Oh, have mercy.

At the benefit, Robert Wells had looked like Lance's father. But now, Julia thought they could have been brothers.

Behind her, she heard Amanda moving through the house, talking on the phone. Caroline and Nina were upstairs, debating the merits of plantation shutters. Only Julia knew that an Academy Award winner stood on their doorstep. She felt the overwhelming need to keep it that way.

"Hello again," he said after no doubt realizing that Julia had temporarily lost the power of speech. "I'm afraid we weren't properly introduced. I'm Robert Wells." His hand was across the threshold, and Julia was grasping it before she really understood what was going on.

"Lance isn't here," she finally managed to mutter. "He's gone. He's on—"

"I know," the older man said with a smile. "I came because I was hoping you might join me for lunch."

Julia looked behind her, fully expecting someone else to be standing there, and then she looked back at him and came dangerously close to mouthing, *Who? Me?*

"You don't have plans, I hope?" he asked.

As he stepped into the marble-covered foyer, Julia didn't feel the need to make excuses. He didn't look at the empty walls and stare, passing judgment on her and her incredibly deficient *girlfriendness*. He just smiled at her, a welcoming smile, a comforting smile, and Julia remembered what Lance had said: "Robert Wells is a very good actor."

But that didn't matter—not to Julia—not right then.

♣

Julia wasn't sure what to expect when Hollywood royalty offers to take you to lunch, but she was thinking along the lines of Spago or Ivy, or maybe some new, hip, ultrasecret place where there are no signs outside and everyone comes in through the alley. Then Lance's father parked his Mercedes on the crowded street and came around to open her door—no valet.

"I hope you're hungry," he said. But after he'd helped her out of the car, he didn't usher her through a dark door where a Prada-clad young man stood with a clipboard, manning a front desk. Instead, he pushed open the glass and steel door that released some of the most heavenly aromas Julia had ever smelled. Inside the small room, two-dozen laminate-covered tables sat between rows of brightly colored plastic benches that ran from the glass storefront to a counter and kitchen in the back.

With a step inside, a man at a nearby table looked up and recognition filled his face. *What are we doing here?* Julia wondered. *He's going to get mobbed,* she thought, but the man in the booth only tilted his head in their direction and said, "Hey, Bob," as if everyone in the joint had an Oscar. Then, Julia looked closer at the diners, thinking that in L.A., even that was possible.

"You come here often?" she asked as Bob steered her toward the counter, where the unmistakable aroma of barbecued ribs was so strong that Julia didn't know if she had the strength to stand and order. She wanted to pull a roasted potato from a passing plate because she felt she might die if she didn't eat something right away.

"This," Bob said dramatically as he pointed to the greasy marquee that hung above the counter, spelling out their culinary options in small plastic letters, "is Rick's. You know *Casablanca*?" he asked, and Julia nodded. "Well, you're about to find out why everyone really comes to Rick's."

Bob ordered for them both—two rib specials. "Not a vegetarian, I'm assuming?" he asked through a grin that, to Julia, was eerily familiar.

"Rancher's daughter," she said, pointing to herself as if claiming a label. "I'd be disinherited if I became a vegetarian."

"Good girl," he said, handing her a plate as he removed his wallet and paid the cashier at the end of the cafeteria-style line. Her lunch with the Hollywood elite had cost him fifteen seventy-five. Tip not included.

She followed him to a table in the back, through a virtual

cross-section of American culture. A pair of college students leaned over open textbooks as they studied with sauce-covered fingers. Two men in three-thousand-dollar suits sat across from each other, speaking with passion in between bites of beans and slaw. An impossibly thin woman in dark sunglasses and a tracksuit sat in the very corner as if hiding from the rest of her Pilates class. None of them looked at Robert Wells.

He must have read her mind because he eased into a booth and said, "No one bothers me here. That's part of the reason I like it."

"Oh," she said, thinking back on her brief brush with fame. For a while, people had known her. Robert Wells had lived with that for three decades—thirty years of belonging in some small way to society at large. She glanced at him. She felt exhausted on his behalf.

"It smells great," she said.

He took a bite. She took a bite, and Julia found herself growing nervous for the first time since he'd stepped inside the house.

"It's funny seeing you actually," she said when the silence was too much. "I was up late last night and the classic movie station was doing an Oscar marathon, and—"

"Don't even tell me," he said, laughing, waving her words away. "Oh, please don't tell me you watched it."

She looked at him, shocked. "Of course I watched it. I've seen it before, of course, but . . . You were wonderful. Of course I watched it."

He sank farther into the booth and a smile spread across his face, as if caught in an old memory he'd half forgotten and only just remembered. "That was a long time ago."

"Not so long," she said.

"Yeah it was." He nodded again, but then the smile seemed to fade as if the sun had gone behind a cloud outside and the bright light no longer washed through the long glass storefront. He looked like Julia felt.

He leaned forward a little more. His voice seemed a little softer. "The fame thing—it doesn't last," he said. "It's not the kind of thing a person should build a life around."

Julia looked down at her hands, rubbed her fingers, and wished she'd brought some lotion. They seemed dry to her—cracking. "I know."

She thought about Sybil, and without thinking, Julia asked, "Do you ever regret winning it—the Oscar?"

He looked at her, but not like she was crazy, which was how she felt. She started to apologize, to backtrack, to explain, but before she could utter a word, he said, "No one's ever asked me that before." She believed it. *Do you regret winning an Oscar?* What kind of question was *that*? But something in the way he sat there made her stay quiet, waiting. He took a long sip of his tea, and when he set it down, he said, "They should have."

She noticed that he didn't answer the question, but as he looked at her across the table, she knew he didn't have to. Fame and success of that magnitude aren't a choice. If they were, everyone would have them. It takes a magical combination of time and space and fate, a heavenly alignment; suddenly, Julia knew why they're called stars.

Robert had both elbows on the table and was holding a spare rib between his hands as if it were an ear of corn. He didn't look at Julia when he asked, "How's he doing?"

When Julia studied him, she realized Robert Wells wasn't an Oscar winner at that moment; he was just a father who hated to resort to spying to gain access to his son.

Julia took a hurried sip of her iced tea, then raised her eyebrows and said, "Great! *Wisdom of Solomon* is getting good—"

"No, Julia," he cut her off and leaned farther onto the table. One of his forearms landed in a glob of sauce, but he was unfazed as he stared at her in a way that might have turned a lesser woman to ash. "How's he handling it?"

Julia thought for a long moment about how she should answer, and that—she saw on the father's face—was answer enough.

"He has *handlers*," she said.

"Agent, manager, publicists, assistants?" he asked but it wasn't really a question. It was more like a memory that he was asking himself if he should relive. "He needs you," he said simply. "Trust me. He needs his family."

"Yeah," Julia said, adjusting the paper napkin on her lap, wondering when and how she became more Lance's family than his father. She picked up her fork and started playing with her food, pretending to eat; though, in truth she'd lost her appetite.

"He hates me, doesn't he?"

"No. No!" She leaned forward and reached for his hand but pulled back at the last moment. "I'm sure that's not—"

"I just hope he isn't becoming me."

What am I supposed to say to that? Julia wondered. Of course he's not becoming you? I hope he's not becoming you, too? Would becoming you really be so bad? She honestly didn't know, so she didn't say anything at all.

"You're a very beautiful woman, Julia," Robert Wells told her and Julia looked at him—dazed. It was the most unexpected compliment she'd ever received and from the most amazing source. "And I *know* beautiful women," he said, smiling.

A blush spread through her cheeks. She tucked a stray strand of hair behind her ears, needing him to see her really and take the compliment back. She felt unworthy of carrying such a burden.

"So, what do you think of Rick's?" Robert asked, holding his hands out wide to gesture at their extremely unopulent surroundings.

Her smile widened as she examined the room in detail, the unpretentiousness of it, the decadent aroma of food. "It's almost like . . ." she started, but then rethought it.

"Go on," he said.

"Home," she found the strength to finish. "It's almost like home." And it was. "Thanks for bringing me."

"Oh." He quickly shoved her thanks away. "It was my pleasure. My wife wouldn't be caught dead eating like this. I'm grateful for the company."

Wife. The word lingered in the air of Rick's like the smell of hickory and the tangy spices of the sauce. She thought of Lance's mother then realized her mistake, that *wife* is a title that can sometimes be exchanged.

"I'm sorry," Julia said when she realized she'd been gaping. "I just didn't know you'd remarried. Lance never—"

"That's okay, sweetheart. He's never met her, actually. Her name is Cynthia. We've been together twelve years." He fumbled in his pocket then held his wallet across the table for her to see. "That's Lily." He beamed at the photo of the blond-haired, beautiful girl. "She's eleven." Then he flipped the photo over to reveal the image of one of the most stunningly beautiful girls she'd ever seen. She had dark hair and olive skin, high elegant cheekbones, and pouty lips. "And this is Tasha. She's fifteen."

Julia looked at him, and he read her confusion. "Before there was a Cynthia, there was a Nadia," he explained. "Tasha's mother was my second wife. She's in Argentina now. She's Russian by birth." He folded the wallet and slid it back into his pocket.

"They're beautiful," she said. "You have a very beautiful family," she nearly whispered.

She leaned back onto the hard bench and felt the meal growing heavy in her stomach as she thought about Lance and the siblings he'd never known, the family that, to him, didn't exist at all.

Chapter Twenty-two

Study your hand to see what your goals will be. It may be a poor hand for gin or a good hand for gin. In any case, have some plan in mind.

From: James Family Farm

To: OK Lady

Subject: Hope you girls are having fun out there

I hope you girls are having fun. Nothing much is new here. Opal Bailey fell and broke her hip so I'm making some bread.

Do you know when you'll be coming home?

Love,

Mom

P.S. Did you get the meat?

Julia had never been unfaithful to anyone before, so she lay awake all night wondering how she was going to tell Lance she'd cheated on him. With his father. She thought about not telling him, but then she knew he'd probably smell the barbecue smoke in her hair even though she'd washed it—see a little sauce stain on her shirt and then she'd crumble under the interrogation.

"I think I have to tell Lance," she admitted the next morning.

"Oh my gosh!" Caroline screeched then ran to hug her sister. "You're going to tell him you love him. This is so great! It's so . . . unprecedented."

Julia pulled away and said, "Thanks, C." She walked around the counter then before she admitted, "But no, that's not it. I think I have to tell him I had lunch with his dad."

"So you don't love him?" Caroline said, shock creeping into her voice.

"Caroline, of course I . . . I mean, it's obvious we're . . . I mean . . ." She looked between Nina and Amanda and Caroline. "He *hates* his dad," she said finally, hoping one of them might see it for what it meant. "Not dislikes a little. Not doesn't get along with. Hate. Actual hate. For his father."

She looked at Nina, who was the child of divorce, who had two failed marriages of her own, and a seed in the back of Julia's mind started to grow, so she slammed the door on the thought, blocking out the light. She picked up a dishtowel and started folding it—perfect folds. She wondered if Caroline might praise her folding ability instead of noticing what she was saying—what it meant. Finally, when Julia couldn't make the corners of the towel any straighter, she said, "I really like his dad."

"Yeah, he's totally hot for an old dude."

"Nina!" Julia snapped. "That's not . . . It's just . . . Lance *hates* his dad!"

"So Lance isn't perfect," Caroline offered, trying to help. "It's not like Steve's perfect. He clips his toenails in bed—as if I want to see that." She had a dozen more complaints—each telling Julia what she already knew—that Steve was a really nice guy who left wet towels on the floor; that he didn't know how to unload the dishwasher or work the car seats or make Caroline feel valued. Steve was a really nice guy.

And that was supposed to be enough.

"So see, Jules," Caroline said, "not everyone is perfect."

"I know that!" Julia bit back. And she did. She loved imperfection. She needed imperfection. Imperfection can be a very, very comforting thing.

"I just . . . I've got to tell him." She hung the dishtowel over the oven door handle. She straightened it. If someone didn't know better, they'd swear a very together person lived there—*if* someone didn't know better. "I've got to figure out a way to tell him."

"Well, that's simple," Caroline said. "Feed him."

"You're a sight for sore eyes," Lance said when she met him at the door.

She hadn't gone too crazy. Really. Okay, so she'd let Nina do her hair, but really Nina had insisted—practically held her down. And so she'd bought a new outfit, but that was just because Caroline needed to see the hip strip for herself, and what kind of sister would Julia be if she didn't go along? And sure, there had been some eyebrow work, but what's with a little tweezer action?

She hadn't gone *too* crazy.

"Look at you," he said, making her spin like a little plastic ballerina atop a jewelry box. "You look . . ." Then he trailed off. He looked around. "What's that I smell?"

"Caroline's here," Julia said. "And she brought meat."

He walked through the house until he reached the dining room. Caroline and Nina had spent an hour on the table, the candles. Julia had spent a day on the food.

"You did all this?" he said, gesturing at the beautiful table.

Julia blushed. "Guilty."

"You cooked." He motioned to all the food. "All this."

Julia felt a surge of pride swelling inside her. *I made a beautiful meal,* she thought. *I can do this. I can be a good girlfriend.*

"I didn't know you cook."

And just like that, the perfect moment ended.

"Lance," she said numbly, "I wrote a cookbook."

Seeing his mistake, he jumped to say, "I know, it's—"

"It was a *New York Times* Bestseller."

"Oh," he said. "Yeah." He smiled and hugged her. "It looks . . . amazing." He rubbed her arms and kissed the top of her head, and Julia thought, *Yes, there, right there.* And in that moment Julia thought she knew what the fuss was about, why people had always sounded so sad when they'd cocked their heads and said, "So, are you seeing anyone?" Julia thought she might be beginning to understand what was so great about being seen. But then Lance said, "Too bad I ate on the plane."

She pulled away from him and looked around the table. Plane food. She was being blown off for plane food! *That* never happened when she was single. She never slaved away over meals, and most of all, she never cared if they went un-eaten.

"Oh, that's fine. It wasn't any work. It will—"

Julia leaned across the table and blew out the candles. Tendrils of smoke spiraled into the air of the dim room. Candles! She couldn't believe she'd lit candles. Were they not the lamest, most desperate, juvenile thing in the world? *How stupid am I*, she wondered; then she contemplated telling Lance that the electricity had been out earlier in the day. He'd probably believe her. She would have said anything to hide how eager she had been to please.

He picked up a green bean from a bowl and ate it like a

French fry. Once upon a time she would have thought it cute; now she wanted to rip it out of his hands and ask why he didn't fill up on green beans on the plane. There were mashed potatoes on the table, too. And roast beef. And bread. It was her all-time favorite meal. She didn't want him to know that about her, though. She didn't want to be any more bare to him than she already was.

Candles! Really?

He sat down at the table and ate another green bean. His bag was at his feet and his clothes were wrinkled. He looked genuinely exhausted—worn. She couldn't blame him for eating on the plane. It was a private plane. She bet they probably had pretty good food.

So she said, "How was the trip?" partly because she wanted to know, partly because she hoped he wouldn't notice how the napkins looked like little fans.

Fan napkins? She should have her NOW membership revoked.

"It was . . ." He seemed to ponder this more than normal. She wanted to tell him that the answer to that question was "Fine." How was your trip? Fine. How are you feeling? Fine? How is school/your job/life in general? Fine.

How was it possible he didn't know that?

She picked up the potatoes and the meat and took them to the kitchen.

When she came back to the table, she reached for the

bread, but Lance caught her arm and said, "Hey!" He pulled her into his lap, wrapping two very strong arms around her. "It looks and smells great. You look and smell great." He whispered, "I missed you," and Julia thought she might lose it. She might cry or scream or just dissolve into him completely. The woman she'd been a year before would have pulled away, but she didn't know what the woman she was now was supposed to do. It scared her so much she started to run, but then she couldn't and that scared her even more, and she sank deeper and deeper into him—a self-perpetuating cycle she didn't have the strength or will to stop.

"Lance . . ." she started, needing to tell him about his dad, and his mom and every other thought that had passed through her mind in the last six months. "Lance, there's something—"

"I'm not here!" Caroline blurted, flashing through the room in a crouch, as if to make herself as invisible as possible. "I'm not here," she sang again, but she *was* there, and the moment was over.

"Hi, Caroline," Lance called to her. "Thanks for the meat!" But she was already gone.

They sat in silence for a long time before Lance said, "Aren't you gonna eat?"

She shook her head. "I eat while I cook."

She felt him nodding. "Oh," he said. "And in answer to your question, my trip was fine." There it was—the answer she'd wanted—but it felt a little anticlimactic now. "But I was really ready to come home." He held her tighter. "Julia"—Lance turned her to face him—"I want you to know what it means to me that you came out here—that you stayed."

He shifted then, placing her in the chair while he stooped and started digging in his bag. "I know how lucky I am, and I know that when I'm with you, it's better. Everything is better."

Julia realized where he was, then—on the floor—on one knee. Her heart started beating faster and faster until it was pounding like a drum. She looked at Lance, but she didn't want to look at him either. He was blushing. He reached for her hand, but instinctively, she pulled away.

"Julia, I know it's been hard for you," he said, "but I want to give you this, to show how serious I am. That, Julia, if it were up to me, you'd never leave. I guess what I'm trying to say . . ." He started again, but Julia couldn't listen. She was too busy focusing on the small velvet box in his palm and the sick feeling growing in her stomach.

She tried to stand, but her legs had stopped working.

"Go ahead," he said. "Open it." He tried to put the tiny box in her hands, but she shook her head.

"Nah-uh."

The hottest star in Hollywood was on one knee asking her to open a velvet box and she was saying *Nah-uh*.

"Julia," he said, breathing an air of frustration as he opened the box himself. Moments later, a small silver key chain was dangling from his forefinger. "Amanda told me you've been taking cabs everywhere, so I leased you a car. You can go to the dealership tomorrow. You can pick out any one you like."

His smile seemed so warm. She wanted to kiss him, and thank him, and tell the world how lucky she was to love such a caring, thoughtful man, but as soon as the panic passed, all Julia could do was wonder how she was going to keep a straight face when she called Pedro and asked him to drive her to the Mercedes dealership. She wondered if the plastic surgeon or the airport would be next.

Chapter Twenty-three

By playing defensively, you are not completely crushed by one bad hand.

W hat are you doing out here?" Nina asked when Julia appeared beside her. The backyard ran to a low rock wall that separated Lance's property from a steep, rock-covered slope. Caroline and Nina were sitting there, a half-gallon of ice cream resting on the table between them as the lights of the city shone below.

Seeing her sister, Caroline half turned, and said, "What is it? What . . ."

Then Julia pulled out the small velvet box.

"OH MY GOSH!" Caroline yelled. "He asked you to marry him!"

Caroline looked at Nina. Nina looked back, and soon they were hugging each other, jumping up and down, and screeching at the top of their lungs. Julia understood about every fourth word.

". . . Vera Wang . . ."

"Guys," Julia yelled, trying to pry them apart.

". . . call Mom . . ."

"Caroline, wait a—"

". . . stuffed mushrooms . . ."

"Stop it!" Julia yelled. She pulled the key chain out of the box and dangled it in front of them—a bright, shiny object. *Here kitty kitty,* she thought.

"What's . . ." Nina started but was unable to finish. She looked at Caroline and then back again, and Julia knew why people lie. She didn't want to break the moment. It had been a good one—for them at least. *So what would it hurt if I let them sample some wedding cake? Who doesn't like cake?*

"Oh," Caroline said, her face falling. "It's a—"

"Car," Julia finished for her.

"No," Nina snapped, wide-eyed. "It's a Mercedes!"

"I thought he was proposing," Julia said numbly, staring into the night. She felt Caroline rub her back.

"Oh, sweetheart, it's—"

"No, Caroline," Julia jumped in. "I thought he was proposing and I almost threw up." And then the panic that she'd felt moments before came flooding back, and this time, she didn't try to stop it. "It really freaked me out," Julia said, trying to catch her breath. "And then I freaked out about freaking out. That's not normal. *I'm* not normal."

"Sure you—" Caroline started, but one look from Julia cut her off.

She was breathing hard with one palm pressed against the stone fence and another to her stomach. "I thought my boyfriend—which is a word I despise, by the way—was going to ask me to marry him, and I had a panic attack. That's not normal. I'm not normal. It was just like the nightmare."

She expected them to say, *Yeah, yeah* and *That's right.* What she got was, "What nightmare?"

"You know," she said, "the you're-standing-in-a-church-in-a-white-dress-and-can't-go-through-with-it dream." She searched their empty faces. *"You know . . ."*

They didn't.

"You know!" Julia tried once more. "That terrible feeling of waking up in the middle of the night sweating and stuff because you either have to marry some loser you don't really love or humiliate yourself and give Aunt Gladys back her blender."

"Aunt Gladys is dead."

"It's just a dream, Caroline!" Julia snapped, and by just looking at them, she could tell she was the only one who'd had it.

A long moment passed as Julia leaned against the wall.

"Don't freak over the presents thing, Jules," Nina said expertly. "If you want to keep the presents, you get married, then get divorced. Divorced people never give the presents back."

Luckily, Caroline stepped forward. "I don't think this is about the presents, Neen."

Julia nodded. "I saw that box and I thought I was going to be sick. Which means, of course, I'm sick."

"No," Caroline soothed. "No. You're right to not want to rush into anything."

"Right!" Julia said, suddenly agreeing, relieved to have something besides her own messed-up psyche to blame. "We're not there yet. He knows that. I know that." She sank to the arm of Nina's chair. "It's just a car."

"No," Nina said again, "it's a *Mercedes*."

They sat in silence, passing the ice cream between them. After a long time she felt Nina shift and say, "The second time I married Jason, we were in Vegas and we'd been there for three days, and you know how, by the third day, Vegas can get pretty boring? So that night Jason looks at me and says, 'Do you want to get married or something?' That's a proposal I said yes to." She took the ice cream from Julia and gestured with the spoon. "Here's a piece of advice for ya—if a proposal ends with the phrase 'or something'—take the something."

Julia nodded. Caroline sighed, and they watched the darkness for a while before Julia said, "I wonder what it would have been—the *or something*."

"I've thought about that a lot, actually," Nina said. "It probably would have been bowling."

"Hum. Yeah, that would have been better," Julia said. "You're a pretty good bowler."

"I know."

Chapter Twenty-four

As in many card games, gin begins with a play by the non-dealer.

From: James Family Farms

To: OK Lady

Subject: A cold one here last night

We had a cold one here last night. Daddy's cutting wood today and Steve and the kids are coming by, so I've got to start cooking.

And I should probably also remind Daddy what happened the last time Steve tried to use the ax.

Julia, do you have wood at your house?

Later and love,

Mom

The next morning Julia was in the bathroom drying her hair when Nina came in. "Come on," she said. "Let's go try on cars."

"Are cars something you really try on?"

"They are when I get them."

Twenty minutes later they were in the rental and Caroline was saying, "I think you should get a convertible—a red one. A two-seater." She smiled and seemed proud, like this was a really big step her therapist had encouraged her to take, then she exclaimed, "No SUVs!" and Julia wondered what kind of juice box emergencies and diaper explosions lay in her sister's sordid, twisted past.

The salesman's name was John, but Julia secretly suspected that sometimes he was *Johnny* or maybe *Jack,* whichever would close the deal. They'd no sooner pulled into the lot than he came striding toward them through the rows of gleaming cars, the sun bouncing off them like the sea. He looked a little like he could walk on water.

"Hello, ladies," he said, and Julia instantly knew that he was working on a screenplay about the seedy underbelly of luxury automotives sales. She just knew he was going to tell her how Lance would be the perfect lead.

"And what can I do *you for* today?" he asked and Julia thought, *Is that funny? Has that ever been funny?*

Nina stepped forward, taking the lead, partially because Nina had grown up on a car lot, and it didn't matter that her dad sold used Fords and Chevys to high school kids in Oklahoma, and *that* was a Mercedes dealership in Beverly Hills. It was still her turf.

John was really good looking—deceptively so—in the way good salesmen always are. Jason, Julia remembered, was in sales. *The Checks* came from commission.

Where's the ugly salesguy? Julia wanted to know. *I want to lease a car from that guy.*

Julia heard a squeal behind her and turned to see Amanda and Caroline opening the doors of a sexy little two-door roadster.

"Ooh," Caroline said as she gripped the leather wheel, "try fitting a car seat in this!"

Nina and John wandered down an aisle of SUVs. Julia saw Nina lean back against one. She heard a very sickening reference that involved "kicking his tires" and thought she was going to throw up.

She strode up and down the aisles. She leaned over the stickers in the windows, but she wouldn't touch the glass, leave fingerprints. *Ooh, thirty-two miles per gallon on the highway,* she said to herself and moved on. *Duel-side air bags,* she sang quietly and kept walking. When she leaned down to look inside a gorgeous sedan, she saw Nina and John in the rearview mirror—being closer than they appeared.

Nina shifted her weight and flipped her hair and used every girl trick Julia had ever seen but never mastered.

When Caroline appeared beside Julia and said, "What's up?" Julia jumped.

But Julia couldn't really answer. She was too busy thinking about Nina's father, the used car king of Northeast Oklahoma. His name was John and he'd been an All-State lineman in high school, and oh yeah, everyone called him Big John.

Nina took after her mother—the size part, not the filled-the-freezer-with-casseroles-then-abandoned-her-child part. Nina wouldn't have known how to make the casseroles.

Nina had hated that car dealership and had run from it as far and fast as she could—first to Jason, then all the way to California. Maybe it was destiny. Maybe love always is. Maybe Nina and John were going to spend the rest of their lives making honest deals on good automobiles at fair prices. She wondered if it was true that all little girls eventually grow up to marry the new versions of their fathers.

Caroline pointed toward a shiny silver sedan and said, "M345 Turbo Coupe for your thoughts?"

Julia pointed between two cars to John standing on the other row, kicking a bumper, showing how it bounced back as Nina gave him her best *you're such a big strong man* eyes.

"Does he remind you of Big John?" Julia asked.

"Nina's dad?" Caroline looked back at John and shrugged. "Maybe a little, I guess. Why?"

"Oh. No reason." Julia shook her head. She shielded the sun from her eyes and looked over the shimmering lot. It wasn't until Caroline turned away that she said, "Lance didn't know what a brush hog was. Remember that?"

"What?" Caroline asked. "What in the world are you talking about?"

"Remember when he came in August? He thought it was an actual pig. He thought we were going to eat it instead of cutting weeds with it. Dad still teases him about it."

"Why on earth would you think about that now?"

One row away, Nina was giggling. She sounded at home.

Julia shrugged. "Do you think most girls eventually end up with men like their fathers?"

Caroline rolled her eyes. She threw her hands in the air. She did everything a person can possibly do to show frustration. "Is *that* what you're worried about? That Lance isn't like Dad so you can't be happy?" Leave it to Caroline to cut to the heart of the matter. "That's ridiculous." She took two quick steps, then spun and said, "After all, Steve is *nothing* like Dad."

Then her cell phone rang and she answered it. After a second she snapped, "No, Steve, I don't care if they are both called detergent, you can't use Tide in the dishwasher!"

"Thanks, Caroline," Julia whispered as she gave her sister a big thumbs-up and backed away. "Big help!"

When Julia turned, she saw a man bolting toward her from the glass-enclosed showroom. He had too much weight around the middle and the mere act of climbing down the stairs brought beads of perspiration to his brow. He opened his mouth to speak, but before he said a word, Julia pointed toward a white sedan—the most boring car on the lot—and said, "I'll take that one."

Chapter Twenty-five

> If you fail to arrange your cards so that you can instantly see your possibilities, you may miss a play, or your hesitation may give away something about your hand.

From: James Family Farm

To: OK Lady

Subject: Turkey Day

Hi girls. Just a reminder that Thanksgiving is next week. Do you need Dad to pick you up at the airport?

You are coming home. Aren't you?

Love,

Mom

"What are you working on?"

Julia looked up from her computer, temporarily disoriented, and glanced around the café. It took her a second to see the guy with the blue Macintosh computer who was leaning his chair back on two legs, talking to her.

How many times had she heard that question? Hundreds. Thousands maybe. But still, Julia had to shake her head a little, wake up, and think, before she could say, "Oh . . . a novel . . . I guess." Her hands felt restless on the keys. Her mind wandered. But the guy in the corner didn't know that. He didn't know her.

"Whoooo, a novelist. That's impressive."

Is it? Julia wondered. *Was that sarcasm?* She looked around, wanting to ask someone, but the café was empty except for an older man who wrote longhand with a red pen on yellow legal pads. He looked like he would have been more comfortable chiseling on stone.

"So what kind of book is it?"

She tried to understand the question—not the words, but the tone. "Oh, um, a romance, I guess."

But then, Blue Macintosh guy—Mac, she decided to call him—shook his head and wrinkled his nose like he'd just sniffed inside a carton of milk that had gone sour. He said, "Nah, you don't want to write one of those."

"I don't?"

"No. You want to do a mystery or a serial killer bit or something. You can throw in some love if you want to, but don't write a 'romance.'" He made imaginary quote marks in the air just in case Julia missed the fact that he was very, very clever.

"Why's that?" Julia said, feeling more amused than angry.

The front legs of Mac's chair hit the floor with a sharp crack. He put his hands on his knees and leaned close to her. He was about to let Julia in on a secret that would change her life—she was about to owe him big time. "You know Hitchcock?"

"Well, not personally," Julia said.

Mac smiled as if he appreciated jest, like maybe he invented the concept.

"Well, old Hitch used to talk about this thing called the MacGuffin. You know about MacGuffins?"

Julia shook her head. Mac smiled. He wasn't expecting her to know, and Mac loved being right. "The MacGuffin is the thing everybody wants—the Maltese Falcon, the letters of transit that can get a guy out of Casablanca no-questions-asked, the blueprints Princess Leia hid in that little annoying robot dude. You following?"

Julia nodded.

"So you don't want to write a romance." He leaned his chair back on its hind legs again. His work there was obviously done.

"And why is that?" she asked.

"Because love makes a terrible MacGuffin."

◆

"Hey," Julia said over the pounding of the heavy bag. She hadn't been to the pool house before then, so she looked around it, amazed. "What does this do?" She pointed at a contraption that probably came standard in your average torture chamber . . . or gym. As far as Julia was concerned, there wasn't much of a difference.

Lance, however, didn't look at her. His fists flew with ease. The bag swayed back and forth. She half expected *Eye of the Tiger* to start playing in the background.

"Hey, Rocky!" she said, catching his attention at last.

He jerked around to look at her then slowly smiled. "Yo, Adrienne."

Cheesy? Yes. But her heart flipped over a little anyway.

She sat down on an exercise bench and watched him punch the bag some more. It was effortless. She'd never seen him do anything quite like it. She'd never seen him do a lot of things. She wondered how it would feel to be like that— good at everything.

The *whack, whack, whack* of his fists stopped briefly. She watched him wipe some sweat from his face, but he didn't smile. He hardly looked at her.

"What's wrong?" she said, sensing something. Still, she was surprised when she saw she was right.

"There's a script going around town," he said, not looking at her, his eyes and fists focused on the bag with laser-like precision. "It's a big deal." Punch-punch. "They want me to star in it." Punch-punch-punch.

"And that's bad because . . ."

And then he caught the bag with one arm and turned to look at her. Sweat poured down his face, his arms. "Guess who they want to costar?"

This wasn't Lance being coy, Julia knew. The answer wasn't exciting. He didn't really want her to guess.

When he released the bag, his punches were slower, but stronger. He was making them count, and something clicked inside Julia. A card turned over. She stopped bluffing.

"I went to lunch with him," she said quickly, needing to be free of the words. "When you were gone." The punches stopped for a second, then they started again—faster this time. "He was very nice. Very . . ." She didn't know what to say, what was right and what was wrong.

"Lance . . ." She stood and stepped toward him, needing him to stop, needing him to turn to her and explain where that anger came from, how deep it ran. How she could keep it from ever being directed at her. "Lance, I'm sorry." Her eyes burned. Her voice cracked, and even over the pounding of the bag, Lance heard it.

"Don't," he said. "You don't have to apologize."

"Yes I do. I mean, I must. I know you hate him, but I don't know how that works. Thanksgiving is next week. Did you know that? And my family—my enormous, intrusive, insane family is going to have lunch at my Aunt Mary's, and my mom is going to bake twelve kinds of pie, and—"

"What are you saying, Julia?"

The punches had stopped, and he was standing there, looking at her. Sweat poured off him, and he was the single most beautiful man she'd ever seen. She knew she'd love him forever, but she couldn't say that. Instead, she just stood there, thinking, *Love makes a terrible MacGuffin.*

"Lance, what are we going to do?" she asked. "About Thanksgiving?" she added as an afterthought. The last thing she wanted was the big answer to that question. She preferred her truths small, bite-sized. That way she could consume them all day and never feel full. "Are you . . . I mean, are we going to go to my family or your family . . ."

Lance was hitting the bag, but he wasn't really hitting it. It was more like an afterthought, playing around a bit. It made Julia want to hurl something at him.

"Lance!" she yelled. "This is a big thing! Big. Very big."

"Okay. Okay," he said, and his voice was calm. He'd punched his rage away, and now he looked at her, concern pouring from him like the sweat. "You can go home and be with your family, or you can stay here, or . . . whatever you want to—"

"No, Lance, no. Not *whatever*. This is big stuff. People get divorced over this stuff—and that's for married people.

Married people have a lot more paperwork. I don't know if you've noticed this or not, but you and I don't have any paperwork!"

"True."

"I'm serious!"

"So am I." He held her by her arms away from him, forcing her to look at him. "Believe me, I know what makes people get divorced."

And then she knew. She knew why she couldn't breathe, couldn't write, couldn't think straight. Julia realized then there was a side of him she didn't know, and it scared her. If he could feel that way about his dad, she wanted to know why. She wanted to know how to keep him from someday feeling that way about her.

"Lance, this thing with your dad is so different from anything I know," she said. "So totally different. And then after that hideous encounter with your mom . . ."

"What about my mom?"

She looked at him, held his gaze. "Oh, she came. It was awkward and strange and . . ."

"And what?"

"And she hated me."

"She did not."

Then Julia looked at him, a piercing look. *"You weren't here."* And he shut up.

She sank onto the bench again and buried her head in her

hands. "I told you this wasn't my game," she whispered as he took a seat beside her.

He put his elbows on his knees, and for the first time since she'd gotten to his gym, he seemed out of breath. Tired. It was a fight neither of them had been training for.

"Where'd he take you?" Lance asked. Then he clarified, "My dad."

"A barbecue place called Rick's."

From the corner of her eye she saw him nod. "Yeah. He always loved Rick's."

That was all he had to say. The fire was gone. And Julia sat there numbly, not knowing what card to play.

"So, is it good?" she asked, and he looked at her, not understanding. "The script?"

Lance glanced away. He nodded. "Wes says it has Oscar written all over it."

"Not literally, though? Right?" she asked, smiling in spite of herself, in spite of everything. "It's not like written on there with Magic Marker or something?"

Lance laughed softly. "No, I don't think so."

"Because if it is, then that copy could have just belonged to some guy named Oscar. That'd be pretty embarrassing."

Chapter Twenty-six

If you are playing a very strong opponent, you must be careful to remember every discard and play.

"Hi," Lance said when he heard his mother pick up. "Thanks for bringing my stuff. Sorry I missed you."

"Oh, hi honey, I'm sorry I—"

"Why were you a bitch to Julia?"

He heard her silence, felt her processing and analyzing and—

"Did she say that?"

"No, Julia wouldn't say *bitch*, Mother. If you *knew* her, you'd know that. Julia says *dang* and *darn* and *drats* and the occasional *damn*—but only on really special occasions. *Bitch* is entirely my word."

"Well, dear, exactly *how* was I a bitch?"

"She is doing for me what you didn't want to do for Dad. It's not her scene either, Mother, to borrow your word, but she is doing it!" He waited for his pulse to slow, his voice to soften. "She's doing it for me—for us. She is sacrificing—"

"Oh, from what I saw, it isn't much of a sacrifice. Lance, that house—"

"You think it's about money," he said. It wasn't a question. It was a realization. "If you think this is even a little about money, Mother, then you *really* don't know her. She has her own money. She has her own life, and she could go back there any second and be a hell of a lot better without the likes of me, but she doesn't because I'm the greedy bastard who keeps asking her to stay!"

Lance had never spoken to his mother that way. Never. And it was equal parts liberating and terrifying. His hand actually shook as it held the phone. His pulse raced, and he didn't know where this new fury was going to take him.

Then, his mother said, "Your father never asked me, you know? To stay?"

Lance processed this, tried to fit it into his memories somewhere between the image of his dad's first movie and the small apartment his mother moved into six months later. He tried to see if that would make the pieces fit better, but they didn't, so he said, "See, I always told you I wasn't anything like him."

"I'm glad he didn't ask, Lance." She spoke slowly—deliberately—as if to remove all doubt. "It's one of the reasons I still love him."

"That's funny." Lance sighed. "It's one of the reasons I hate him."

They both sat for a long time in the silence of people who know they've already said too much.

Finally, Lance said the thing that had made him pick up the phone. "Her family is all in Oklahoma. Family is really big for Julia, but she's staying out here for Thanksgiving—for me. She wants to do a meal. She wants to—"

"Do you want me to come to Thanksgiving, darling?"

"Yeah. Yeah, I do."

"Then I will," she said. "On one condition."

"Okay."

"Ask your father."

The pool furniture came. Nina had gotten it from the estate of a former costume designer for MGM who had a half-century's worth of chiffons and silks squirreled away in old milk crates and cardboard boxes. The chairs were wrought iron with cushions that, even though they needed reupholstering, had held the bikini-clad bottoms of stars like Sophia Loren and Elizabeth Taylor back when stars were stars. Those lounge chairs knew how to hold a woman with some meat on her bones, but still Julia didn't feel like trying them.

"Come on. The sun will do you good," Nina said.

"The sun kills, Neen. Slowly. But first, it makes you ugly," Julia corrected.

"You can practically still see Sophia Loren's butt imprint in the cushions. You're too good for Sophia Loren now?"

So Julia lathered on the SPF 45 and took a seat. Nina didn't join her, though, so Julia was alone with her thoughts and the beautiful day and Sophia Loren's butt indentation that was still significantly smaller than Julia's. She looked at the pool, at the city below, and at the clear blue horizon with its wisps of clouds that drifted slowly across the sky, and there, without a care or worry in the world, something occurred to her: *Something's wrong.* It was a feeling like maybe she'd left an iron on, but it was bigger than that—nagging. Like maybe her whole life could catch fire.

Then she went through the checklist of her life. Healthy friends and family: check. Financial security: check. Boyfriend on the cover of *Vanity Fair*: double-check. There was nothing in the world that she should rightfully want or need, and yet the nagging feeling lingered, so all Julia could do was look out over Lance's million-dollar view and think, *How greedy am I?*

"There you are." Caroline sank into the chair beside her. She pushed up the sleeves of her shirt and closed her eyes, basked in the sun without a thought of wrinkles or sun spots or cancer. Julia vowed to be a little more like Caroline—right up until the point when her sister said, "I married a moron."

"What did Steve do?" Julia asked.

If it's possible for someone to roll her eyes when they're closed, Caroline did it.

"Oh, he's already called five times today in a panic because the laundry hasn't done itself while I've been gone." She sounded proud of herself, assured. "So I told him to do it."

"How did that go?" Julia asked.

"Well"—Caroline straightened and looked at her—"then he calls back in twenty minutes, saying the washing machine is broken and he wants to know where we keep the warranty information. He starts complaining because he's going to have to get someone to come fix it."

"And . . ." Julia prompted, knowing Caroline was waiting for it, milking the story for all it was worth.

"I asked if he was *sure* it was broken and he said, 'Yes, Caroline, I graduated top of my class from Virginia Law. Of course I know when a washing machine is broken.'" Caroline paused to roll her eyes, no doubt resisting the urge to remind the world who had put him through law school, but at the moment, that was beside the point. "So I asked him what it was doing, and he said it wasn't filling up with water—that anyone who has made partner at a top law firm knows washing machines are supposed to have water, and that all he needs from *me* is the warranty info."

She leaned back on the lounge and shielded the sun with her hands. Julia wondered how long her sister would be content to stay like that. Maybe an hour. Maybe a day. Maybe forever.

"It was the dryer, wasn't it?" Julia asked.

"Yup."

"He didn't apologize, did he?"

"Nope."

As Caroline lay there, soaking up the California rays, Julia saw a small smirk grow on the corner of her sister's lips, and she knew that despite what Caroline said, this trip wasn't a sabbatical—it was a game of chicken, and Caroline wasn't about to blink.

Julia watched her sister, trying to work up the nerve to say, *Go home*. But she couldn't. Caroline looked so happy and Julia was never one to tell someone she should look miserable—even if she was.

They were alone, and finally, Julia couldn't help herself. "Caroline, did you leave Steve?"

Caroline bolted upright. "No!" she snapped. Her face was hard. Her cheeks were red. "I told you, it's a—"

"Sabbatical?"

"Yes!" Caroline said. "I told you that." Then she softened. "I'm trying out his life for a while. He's trying out mine."

It sounded good, but there was a fatal flaw Julia didn't want to point out—*this isn't Steve's life*. Steve was a tax attorney for a downtown firm. He wrote briefs. He worried about tax codes. He knew what *Fiduciary* meant. Twice a year he had to pretend he liked golf long enough to go on the firm retreat with the other partners, but mostly he just went to the office every day and kept getting stronger glasses. *This isn't Steve's life.*

"Caroline, I'm not asking to be nosy, all right. But do you ever think about divorce?"

"Divorce?" Caroline said then exclaimed again, "Divorce!" She shook her head. She waved the word away as if it was completely impossible, against the laws of nature. "Never," she said in a way that made Julia know she'd never ask again. Then Caroline leaned back and closed her eyes. "Murder?" she said. "All the time."

They lay side by side in the sun for a long time. Julia could almost close her eyes and imagine they were little girls again, on blankets in the backyard, before doctors and beauty magazines broke the news that suntans are terrible things. All they needed was Madonna singing from a scratchy cassette and they could have been kids again. But then Julia heard Caroline say, "Do you remember Robbie Miller's wedding?"

Julia nodded her head but didn't have a clue why Caroline would choose that moment to reminisce about her third cousin's wedding.

"Remember how they had those huge, pretentious candelabras, and those hideous invitations, and how we got there late so we had to sit in the very back?"

"Yeah, but Caroline—"

"Remember how we got in trouble during the ceremony?"

Julia rolled her eyes as she realized where her sister was going. "I did *not* openly heckle during the lighting of the unity candle."

Caroline smirked. "I believe your exact words were—and I quote—*'Unity candle, are you freaking kidding me? Keep you own flame, honey. Don't let him blow it out'*—unquote."

"I didn't shout."

"The minister asked us to leave."

Julia knew when she was beaten.

"So, what is it then?" she asked when she saw the dark shadow that ancient memory had brought to her sister's face.

"I let my flame go out."

Then Julia nodded, finally starting to understand.

Chapter Twenty-seven

> As you analyze the play of the hand in rummy, you'll find it's not the simple game of luck it may appear.

From: James Family Farm

To: OK Lady

Subject: cooking

Just cooking up a storm here, today. Aunt Mary said she doesn't need bread, but I thought I'd make some hot rolls. Just in case.

Everyone loves hot rolls.

Should I save you some?

Love,

Mom

W hat are you looking for?" the waitress asked as Julia sat in the Fade Inn, searching online cookbooks for the perfect holiday meal. She needed it to be perfect. No other adjective would do.

"I'm cooking Thanksgiving dinner," Julia said. "It's for my boyfriend's family." Then she glanced up at the girl. "I hate that word," she confessed. "*Boyfriend*. But what else can I say, *manfriend*? That sounds like I should be in a nursing home, hoping he'll let me take whiffs off his oxygen tank. I don't think I like the word *manfriend*." She might as well have been talking to herself at that point, but the waitress was still there. Then for reasons she didn't know she heard herself say, "I'm kinda scared."

"Yeah." The girl's face broke out into a broad smile. "People freak out around the holidays." The young woman shrugged then looked down at Julia, studied her. "I broke up with a guy on Thanksgiving one time." She refilled Julia's drink and sat down in an empty chair. The coffee shop was especially empty and quiet. The only sound was Mac in his dark corner, banging away on the keys.

"Really?" Julia asked. "Why?"

"He showed up with a date."

"You're kidding!"

"Yeah. To *my* Thanksgiving dinner." The waitress leaned back in her chair and grabbed a cup off the counter behind her. She took a sip. "But it could have been worse, I guess."

"Really?"

"Yeah. He'd told her I was his *ex*-girlfriend, and she made a pumpkin-flavored cheesecake. So imagine me slaving away on turkey and crap and this girl making this nine-thousand-calorie cheesecake, and for what? A big scene at the door that the idiot hadn't even seen coming where *I* broke up with him, and then *she* broke up with him."

"What happened?"

"We went inside and ate the cheesecake." She took another sip. "I still have the recipe if you want it."

"Sure," Julia said. "That sounds good."

And then she started crying.

Julia didn't know where the tears came from or why, but it felt good to set them free.

"Hey," the waitress said. "Hey, it's okay." She leaned forward, touched Julia's hand. Her fingers smelled like coffee.

"I'm so sorry," Julia said. "I don't know . . ." She stammered. "I don't know what's wrong with me." Then she looked up at her. "Do *you* know? You used to be a therapist, right?"

But the woman shook her head. It wasn't going to be that easy. "What do *you* think is wrong with you?"

Julia shrugged. Why did personal growth have to require so much effort? Why couldn't it just happen—like regular growth? She could put on twenty pounds without even thinking about it. Shouldn't this be the same way?

"You're a bright woman, Julia," the waitress said. It was a voice of education and confidence and two hundred dollars an hour—not eight seventy-five plus tips. "Surely you have some idea."

This time Julia shook her head, side to side, as if she were a little girl. As if she didn't want to open up and say "Awwww." As if she just didn't want to open up.

"Julia—" the woman started, but by then Julia had found her words.

"I don't want to be jealous all the time."

When the tears started again, the woman leaned across the small table and pushed a shiny silver napkin dispenser toward Julia, who took one and blew her nose. The paper was rough against her skin. It crumbled. "I don't want to feel like maybe I'll start crying in random places for no good reason. I want to know . . . I want to know why I can't shake the feeling that something is wrong—like I'm wrong or . . ." She played with the fraying napkin in her hands. "I don't know."

"Who are you jealous of?"

"What?" Julia asked, shaking her head, wondering where the question had come from.

"You said you didn't want to be jealous all the time. Of whom are you jealous?"

"Oh, I don't . . ." But the answers were all around her, from Sadie Whitaker's face in bookstore windows to the people working around her, trying to write the next big Oscar contender, unaware of the drama playing out ten feet away. They knew what they wanted, and they wanted what she had. But all Julia could do was pull another napkin from the dispenser and face the fact that she would have traded the having for the knowing in a heartbeat.

"I used to be . . ." She leaned forward, glanced side to side. "I used to be sort of famous."

"I know." The simplicity of the words—the sheer certainty of them—knocked Julia back. "You're Julia James. I used to recommend *Table for One* to my suddenly single support group. It was a big hit."

"Really?" Julia asked. "You knew?"

The waitress smiled, but didn't answer. Instead, she leaned forward as if it were her turn to share a secret. "You know, it's okay to not have the answers sometimes, Julia."

"I know that," Julia said.

"Do you?"

Julia nodded and blew her nose again. The ease and comfort of the quick release was gone, and she glanced around now, conscious of her red eyes and runny nose, certain the stares would start at any second and then she'd have to leave that place—her safe place—forever and call Pedro to come drive her someplace else where she could just be "that strange woman who is always alone" as opposed to "that strange woman who cried that one time."

"Do you trust Lance?"

Julia looked up, her session temporarily forgotten in her

haste to cover up what had been momentarily exposed. She shook her head quickly, sending those thoughts flying away as she said, "What?"

"Do you trust him? Do you think he'll hurt you?"

"No," Julia said softly then exclaimed, "No! Lance would never intentionally—"

"Do you think he might hurt you *unintentionally*?"

But Julia didn't answer, didn't dare speak her greatest fear aloud. She didn't think he would, but she knew he had the power to, and it was the most terrifying thing Julia had ever done—giving someone else veto power over her own happiness. She thought back to Nina's lessons, wished she could pick all her cards back up because, once they're out there, *anyone* can do *anything* with them.

When Julia couldn't answer, the waitress-slash-therapist stood and picked up her pot of coffee. It had grown cold sitting there. It would have to be thrown away.

"You're gonna be okay, Julia." Her voice was soft and patient—the voice of someone who has seen it all. Then she pulled a rag from her apron and wiped the table where the pot had been. "I'll get you that recipe if you want."

Julia nodded, acted brave and strong and like ninety seconds before she hadn't been crying like a baby. "That'd be great." But her voice deceived her. It cracked a little, but the waitress—veteran that she was—pretended not to notice. She shifted on her feet, probably remembering why screenwriting had sounded good once, why she'd walked away from the leather couch forever.

"There's nothing really wrong with you, Julia. Everyone cries. Everyone gets jealous." She pushed her chair back beneath the table. She was saying time was up. Her next appointment would be walking in at any moment.

Julia tried to nod, to smile, then as the young woman stepped away, Julia blurted, "I didn't have a Ken doll. I had a Barbie . . . but no Ken. Do you think that might have messed me up?"

The young woman glanced back. "Barbie messed everybody up."

Chapter Twenty-eight

Whenever you can't decide why your opponent picks up a discard, you should be on the lookout for the card that will tell you the whole story.

From: James Family Farm

To: OK Lady

Subject: Happy Thanksgiving

Happy Thanksgiving, girls. Mary has already called, asking about you. I told her you were spending today with Lance's family.

I'm worried that my hot rolls aren't going to rise, so I think I'll make some biscuits, too.

Mary told Aunt Beverly that she didn't have to bring anything, but she's making a cream pie anyway. I just hope nobody ends up in the hospital this time.

Love,

Mom

haw the turkey. Bake the pies. Peel the potatoes. Pray. Julia had the order down, but something still felt wrong, like maybe it should take more than a year to go from sitting at the kids' table to being the one who cooks the turkey. Like maybe she was playing house, making believe. Like maybe she'd come too far too fast and, as a result, hadn't really gone anywhere at all.

She thought back. She remembered the lean years when she'd been living in New York and hadn't been able to afford the plane tickets home, but she'd been too proud to take money from her parents. "Sorry, I've got to work on Friday," she'd lied. "I just can't make it this year," she'd said. "Actually, my boss has invited me to her house. I'm bringing the cranberries." But there was no lunch, no cranberries, only turkey dinners from Lean Cuisine and lots of football on TV.

As she sat at Lance's new dining room table, she ran her hands over the rich red tablecloth, fingered the fragile china that Nina had arranged a dozen different ways, and tried not to compare those Thanksgivings with this one. Then she'd had a Formica-covered table and a plastic tray. Now, she had a page from *Martha Stewart Living*. Then, she'd had frozen potatoes and processed poultry; now she had a homemade feast and three types of pie. Then, she'd had only one person to feed and please and entertain; then she'd had herself. Then, that had been enough.

It was something to be thankful for.

"Okay," Nina said, appearing behind her. "I think we've got it down. I'm gonna keep Lance's mom away from Lance's dad; Caroline is supposed to keep Lance's dad away from Lance; and Amanda is in charge of keeping Lance's mom away from you." She smiled. She'd been working at it for a while—Julia could tell. If all went well, she might just go pro. For a fee, Nina Anders could set your table and referee your family fights. She was going to make a mint.

"We're all equally in charge of Sybil," Nina added. She didn't wink, but she could have.

"Thanks, Neen," Julia said eventually. "That sounds good."

They walked together to the kitchen, where pots simmered and bread rose. It looked like Thanksgiving. It smelled like Thanksgiving, but somehow Julia knew that everything in her mother's kitchen would taste better.

Amanda came in and asked, "Is Caroline still on the phone?"

Then they all glanced toward the entertainment room, where sounds of marching bands and perky early morning anchors were giving the world another reason to be thankful—helium and great big trailers covered with tissue. They heard Caroline say, "Yes, sweetie, I do see Snoopy," and they jerked their gazes away like people who'd been caught staring.

"How long has she been on the phone?" Amanda asked.

Julia pinched a piece of dough from the glob in front of her. "Since the parade started."

"How long you think she's gonna be on?" Amanda asked again.

"Until the parade ends."

From the other room, they heard, "Look, Cassie, this band is from Oklahoma! Look, sweetheart."

"I can't listen to this," Nina said, going to slide the pocket doors of the entertainment room closed, and for the first time it occurred to Julia how Caroline's "sabbatical" must have seemed to Nina. She wondered if Caroline had left a freezer full of casseroles. But Nina's mom never called with a play-by-play of the Macy's Thanksgiving Day Parade, Julia knew. Nina's mom hadn't called—period.

"She must miss her kids a lot," Amanda said when they were alone.

"Yeah." Julia smiled. "Caroline is a great mom."

"You're gonna be a great mom, too," Amanda said. Julia froze. "I mean—someday," the girl added, quickly back-tracking. "I guess I'm just sad that she's sad—that she didn't go home if that's what she wanted."

What she wants is to be asked to come home, Julia thought, but she didn't say it. It was the kind of truth best never said aloud.

"Amanda, are you sure you don't want to be with your

family today? It must be a holiday for you. You don't have to work."

"But you guys are my family," Amanda said, her eyes as bright and clear and beautiful as the sky outside.

♣

"Everything smells great, Jules," Lance said, and Julia thought, *Since when does he call me Jules?* "And it's not like I'm complaining," Lance began, as again, he surveyed the kitchen counters. There were three pies and two cakes. Eight-dozen hot rolls sat rising on the table in the breakfast room, and five pounds of potatoes were peeled and sliced and sitting in water, waiting to boil. "But do you really think we can eat all this?" His eyes were flirtatious. He was teasing her, coaxing her, and Julia thought that she might cry.

I love you, she wanted to say.

I love you, too, she wanted to hear.

But instead she heard an eerie *"Hellooooo!"*

Sybil appeared at the back door and pushed her way inside. "Happy Thanksgiving, darlings!" She hugged and kissed Nina, then Amanda. Then she came to Lance. "Oh, and you must be the big, strong man I've been hearing so much about." She held a hand out, palm down, inviting him to kiss it. "Sybil Dubois."

Lance looked at Julia. "You never said she was Sybil Dubois!" He looked back at Sybil, kissed her hand then her cheek. Nina looked at Julia like, *Did you put him up to this?* But Julia was as dumbfounded as the next person when he said, "I've seen *The Undead Deception* about a million times."

"You have?" Julia asked.

"Are you kidding?" Lance said in awe. His arm draped around Sybil's shoulder as if she were a national treasure. "That's a classic!"

In unison, Amanda, Nina, and Julia all said, "It is?"

"Ms. Dubois, I can't tell you how thrilled I am to have you here. Can I hug you again?" He didn't wait for an answer. He squeezed her tight. Julia had never seen him starstruck, but there he was. He didn't seem to realize that she'd been right next door all the time.

"Tell me, Lance dear," Sybil said when Lance pulled away, "would you like to see my new goat?"

As Lance held the door for Sybil, Nina inched toward Julia and said, "You know, it's kind of like being home."

The doorbell rang. Moments later, Amanda was darting into the kitchen, saying, "Wes is here."

"I didn't know we invited Wes," Nina said.

"We didn't."

When Wes walked into the kitchen, he didn't look like someone who was ready for Thanksgiving—he looked like someone who was celebrating Thanksgiving in a Hallmark Hall of Fame movie. He wore a designer suit. He had on silver cufflinks. He kissed Julia's cheeks—plural—Wes was a man who could pull off the double-cheeker. Then he handed her a bouquet of white calla lilies. "If only they were as beautiful as our hostess." Wes leaned down to smell the cooling pies. Then, he searched the room and said, "Where's Lance?"

"He's out back with Sybil Dubois," Amanda said.

"Who?" Wes asked, but didn't seem too interested in the answer. He was looking around, his eyes darting through the room as if they might light on the Holy Grail. "So, am I the first to arrive, or . . ."

"Robert Wells isn't here yet, Wes," Julia said. "If that's what you're asking."

"Oh," Wes said, faking surprise. "Oh, Lance's dad is coming? Well, that's nice. Great. Terrific." Wes might not have been a great actor, but he could read a room. Seeing the look on Julia's face, he gave up the charade, leaned onto the kitchen counter and said, "Lance has got to do this movie." He seemed exhausted. He seemed beaten. He was looking for an ally, and Julia, somehow, was it.

"He's not going to find anything like it, and if he turns it down, someone else is going to get this part and then Lance is going to be the idiot who turned it down. Plus"—Wes drew a haggard breath—"this thing with his dad sucks. You know that, right? I don't like to meddle in my clients' lives, but I like Lance." He straightened and looked around the kitchen. Somehow in the last few days that big empty house had started looking a little like home. It was waiting for a family, and Julia was doing her best to bring it one. Wes must have seen it, too, because he rubbed her back and said, "You're doing a good thing here."

The doorbell rang. Sybil screamed, and Julia knew that somewhere in the next yard over, a goat was passing out cold, playing dead. Julia totally knew the feeling.

◆

The silence in the foyer was deafening. As someone who had spent a good deal of her life in the study and pursuit of profound phrases, Julia had always hated that one—a little. But standing on the marble floor beneath the cathedral ceiling as the staircase spiraled skyward to her right, all Julia could do was look at the band of people assembled there and think, *The silence is deafening.*

Even their breathing seemed to echo.

Lance's father stood with his new family just inside the door; his arm was around the woman who must have been wife number three, a statuesque blonde who was the kind of forty-year-old who could make twenty-five-year-olds feel fat, ugly, and generally loathsome. To her right was a mini-her, a string bean of an eleven-year-old with long, thin blond hair and arms and features so delicate they bordered on frail.

But the oldest girl, Tasha, was perhaps the most perfectly beautiful specimen Julia had ever seen. Everyone stared at her. Gay, straight, male, female, it didn't matter. She was going to be turning heads for the rest of her life, and having never known life otherwise, she never noticed. She was immune to her own beauty.

Lance, this is your sister.

But no introductions happened. The whole party stood in that massive, empty foyer as if that was all that existed of the house—Robert and his new family looking at their long-lost member, and him looking back.

Lance, this is your family.

"Hello, everyone."

Julia jerked. It took her a moment to see that the sliver of light had grown wider across the foyer floor, to notice the shadow inside it, and to realize who was talking. "Bob, darling," Donna Collins said, "Happy Thanksgiving, dear."

And just like that the whole room changed. With the cold marble floor and vase of calla lilies by the staircase, it had been about as warm as your average mausoleum, but the mere sound of Donna's voice brought a light to Bob's face, a charge of energy to the room.

"Come here, you!" Bob said, stepping away from his third wife to hug his first. But it wasn't just a hug; he threw his arms around her and lifted her off her feet and held on so tightly it was as if they were getting ready to jump out of an airplane and she had the parachute.

When he put her down, she patted her hair into place and looked around the stunned room. People still weren't talking. This time, for an entirely different reason. Julia cut Nina a look that was meant to ask, *Are divorced people supposed to act like that?* Nina sent her own look back: *Beats the heck out of me.*

Donna walked to Lance then and reached up to kiss his cheek. "Happy Thanksgiving, dear."

He mumbled something in response, but he looked like he wanted to run—away from his parents, the reminder of how things used to be and might have been. Away from the new wife and two sisters who were living, breathing reminders that loving someone isn't enough to earn a happily ever after.

"Hello, you must be Cynthia," Donna said to wife number three, and Robert jumped.

"Oh, forgive me," he said, then he introduced the two halves of his family.

Julia wondered if she'd made enough potatoes and gravy to hold them all together.

Chapter Twenty-nine

Notice the peculiarities of your opponent. When you know the type of game your opponent plays, you are in a better position to outwit him.

Charlie Spozack!" Sybil said, slapping her knee with glee. "Now there's a name I haven't heard in an ice age." She leaned close to Robert Wells and said in a too-loud whisper, "He was a spicket!"

They were in the uncomfortable-furniture-nobody-ever-sits-in room, which was appropriate—nobody was comfortable.

Lance's gorgeous sisters were at a game table in the corner of the room. Lance stood nearby beside the fireplace. The rest of the group had distributed itself equally between the sofas and chairs, and from where Julia stood by the door, she could have sworn that Hercule Poiroit was going to walk in at any minute and tell them all *who'd done it*.

For a long time, not even Sybil had anything to say, or *scream*. Nina was too star-struck; Amanda was too awe-struck; and everyone else seemed dumbstruck.

"Lance knows George Clooney!" Nina blurted.

"That's amazing!" Caroline chimed with way too much fake enthusiasm to fool a room full of people with the the-ater in their blood. Julia could have hugged them both for the effort, but it was too late.

"So," Julia said, pulling her palms together, "can I get anyone a drink? I have iced tea."

"I would love some tea," Bob said, looking like a man who'd give his right arm for a gin and tonic.

"Red wine for me," Cynthia said, easing back, not pick-ing up the hint that Julia had an entirely different definition of *drink*. Good Baptist girls from Oklahoma always do. In-stantly, Julia remembered where she was. She realized her mistake.

"I'm so sorry. I just didn't think to get any wine. I didn't—"

"Julia doesn't drink, Cynthia," Lance said, speaking for the first time in what seemed like hours.

But Lance's stepmother only scoffed. "Everyone drinks. What are you, pregnant?"

If the room hadn't already been moving at the kind of pace that can only been seen through time-lapse photography, that would have stopped them cold. "No," Julia finally muttered then repeated with an emphatic, "No!"

"A.A.?" Cynthia questioned.

"No," Julia snapped.

"Well, then—" Cynthia started, but Bob's hand was on her knee, cutting her off.

"I just love tea, Julia." He started to stand. "Let me help you with that."

"No," Julia said quickly, rushing out. "I've got it." She cut Caroline and Nina a *follow-me* look and then headed out the door.

"Is it just me, or is Lance's dad kind of . . ." Caroline started.

"Hot," Nina finished. "Lance is gonna look like that."

"I know," Caroline said. "But taller."

"Yeah," Nina jumped to agree.

"Excuse me!" Julia snapped. "Before we start worrying about the next forty years, may I suggest we make it through the next four hours?"

"I don't know," Caroline said, glancing at Nina for backup. "I think things are okay. The first time I met Steve's parents, I broke the bathroom."

"What?" Julia said. "Do you mean the toilet?"

Caroline's cheeks turned red as she climbed onto a barstool. "No, I mean the whole room. It started with a towel bar and then . . ." She started straightening a dish-towel in the great James family nervous habit tradition. "I don't want to talk about it."

"See!" Nina said. "No structural damage! We're off to a great start."

From the other room they heard a deafening scream, and Caroline said, "Sybil seems to be having a good time."

♠

"I really hope everyone's hungry," Julia said as Caroline distributed the drinks. *"Because that turkey smells—"* Caroline started but couldn't finish because Donna Collins said, "I'm a vegetarian."

Julia felt herself stop cold as she stood hunched over, tray in hand. Over Wes's shoulder she saw Lance standing by the fireplace, and she shot flames at him with her eyes. "Lance," Julia said slowly, *"can I see you for a second?"*

They made it all the way to the kitchen before Julia yelled, "She's a vegetarian!"

She was literally shaking. Sure, he might have been the one with the personal trainer, but she was the one ready to do bodily harm.

"I should stab you with this!"

"It's a meat thermometer."

She shook as she spat, "So!" Then she tossed it into the sink with a thunk.

"You see me thawing a turkey. You see me making gravy. You personally witness not one but two bacon grease incidents, and you never think to mention that your mom's a vegetarian!!!"

Lance looked sheepish as he said, "Oops."

"Where's that thermometer?" She started past him, but he grabbed her, spun her around, and locked her in some kind of death grip.

"It's okay, Julia. Mom's not going to freak about this. You don't need to freak about this."

"My parents send us half of a dead cow, and you couldn't mention that your mother is morally opposed to meat!"

"Julia." Lance's voice was calm, even. "It's okay. She's not going to care. I eat meat. I've eaten meat my whole life. It's a nonissue." He released his grip and pushed her back toward the room.

Stepping inside, Julia was starting to believe that everything might just be okay. Then, the doors slid open and she saw Lance's beautiful blond sister standing in the center of the room, yelling indiscriminately in the way that is only really allowed between the ages of ten and fourteen.

"Turkeys are abused!" Lily was screaming. "They're raised in factories and made to eat their own filth."

"Lily, sit down," Bob said.

But the girl was bouncing as she jabbed, "I'm not gonna eat it. You can't make me eat it."

"Lily," Bob said, his voice like barbed wire, "sit down!"

"Lily," Donna said, moving toward the girl, offering a matronly arm, "part of having opinions means respecting others' opinions."

Julia was moving toward the girl. "That's fine, Lily. That's fine."

The child's lip was quivering as if she were working up a good supply of tears, and Julia knew that either she was taking her newfound political/social/and dietary activism very seriously or the theatrical apple hadn't fallen far from the tree—all while her father looked ashamed and her mother searched her purse for a silver flask, which she emptied into her iced tea. Wordlessly, Sybil held her own cup toward her, and Cynthia shared.

"Julia, I'm so—" Bob started.

"That's fine," Julia said. "The culture here is different. I know. I should have checked with you before I planned a turkey."

"I can see where that would have come as a surprise," Nina said. *"On Thanksgiving."*

"Lily, you don't have to eat the turkey," Julia soothed.

"I will not sit at a table with murdered animal flesh," the child spat.

"Then you will not sit at the table, young lady," Robert Wells said, and Lance audibly scoffed.

"Looks like someone read *Parenting for Dummies*," Lance said.

"Lance!" his mother bit at him. "Are you one of the children?"

Julia glanced around the room—looking for some sign of sanity—but Nina and Caroline were watching as if they wished they had popcorn; Wes was staring as if his big shot at Oscar was going up in smoke, and Sybil probably hadn't been capable of sanity for a very long time.

"Julia"—she turned to see Robert coming toward her, shame and a plea for forgiveness on his face—"I am so sorry. Lily is going through a little—"

"I'm right here!" the girl chided.

"—phase."

"Really," Julia said. "Really, Robert, today is about family. I don't want to exclude any family members," she said. "And really, there is so much food. I mean, I have sweet potatoes, and mashed potatoes, and gravy."

"There's meat in the gravy, isn't there?" Lily asked, crossing her arms as if Julia wasn't going to slip anything passed her.

"Well, I suppose there is," Julia admitted. "But we have the potatoes and the—"

"I've been on the South Beach for two years," Cynthia

said as she took another swig of her toxic tea. "Even the sight of a potato makes me hurl."

Classy.

"Okay," Julia said, growing as red as her hair. "There's plenty of food. Like the green beans."

"The green beans have bacon in them!" Nina yelled into the fray. Julia spun and gave her a look of instant death, but Nina only raised her hands and said, "They were going to see it eventually."

"Julia," Lance said softly, placing his hand on her arm. "Come on, this is—"

"This is *family*, Lance. This is about family. And being *thankful*," she spat before rushing to the kitchen. "And we're going to be thankful! Do you hear me?"

♣

"Dear God, thank you for this wonderful meal," Lance said, and Julia wanted to shrink and disappear. Her eyelids fluttered between open and closed as she looked at the table covered with hot rolls, cranberry salad, mushroom caps, and a tub of cottage cheese that Amanda had found in the back of the refrigerator. She felt pretty sure that Lance could have been struck down that very moment for lying to God.

"Amen," Lance said.

"Amen," Bob repeated.

Then silence fell over the table as everyone stared at the

motley band of dishes and the twelve virtual strangers with whom they were supposed to share them. Julia felt the entire table staring at her as if to say, *You got us into this mess, now do something.* And she tried not to think about what the James clan was doing right that minute in Oklahoma.

"So, Tasha, I'm so glad you were able to spend Thanksgiving with us," Julia said, turning to the dark-haired girl. "I'm sorry your mother couldn't join us for the holiday."

It was Julia's sweet voice, her *I'd be happy to stay late and clean your erasers if that means you'll like me* voice.

But Tasha was unimpressed. She merely rolled her eyes and said, "My mother is in Argentina. They don't have Thanksgiving. Only *Americans* need Thanksgiving."

She didn't say "*have* Thanksgiving," she'd said "*need* Thanksgiving," and Julia didn't see it as coincidental. Only in America, one of the richest countries in the world, would people have to designate a day to be thankful, as if gratitude were allowed only one three-hundred-sixty-fifth of the time.

Julia smiled weakly then turned to Lance's mother. "So, Donna, what do you have in production at the moment?"

Lance's mother wiped her mouth and said quietly, "*A Christmas Carol* right now and then *Death of a Salesman* starting in January."

"Oh, I was in *Death of a Salesman* once," Sybil said. "But I must say I didn't care for it. No real screaming."

Lance beamed at her. "That's great, Mom. I know how you love that one."

"Now, *Demons at Dusk,*" Sybil said with a nod of approval, "that's a story a woman can scream about."

"That's great, Don," Robert chimed, his elbows resting comfortably on the table. "No one does *Salesman* like you. Hey," he said, "do you remember that time up in Portland when—"

But he didn't finish because Donna had started laughing, and soon he joined in. "Oh," she said, wiping at her eyes. "That was great."

Julia looked between Lance's father and mother and realized that, despite divorce and separate lives, they still had sentences that didn't need finishing, stories so funny that even without the punch line one of them could make the other laugh out loud. And suddenly Julia wanted to know how that could happen. Then, just as suddenly, she *knew.* They weren't some mismatched couple that had grown bitter and hard with time. They had parted ways before the hate could start.

Julia had always thought that finding your great love meant living life together—she'd never known that keeping it might mean living life apart, and suddenly, Julia found herself scooting away from the table. "I . . . I . . . I need to get the . . ." She stood and backed away. "Excuse me."

♥

"Excuse me, Julia—"

"What can I do for you, Donna?" Julia asked, feigning composure when she didn't want that woman in her kitchen—*no, Lance's kitchen,* she reminded herself, feeling raw and exposed, bleeding in front of the last person she wanted to see.

Oh, you're loving this, Julia thought, seething underneath, drawing on every ounce of composure in her body not to scream or fight or melt away, another broken person in a city of lost dreams. *You win,* she wanted to say. *Are you happy now?* But words didn't come as she stared numbly ahead.

"We're out of bread," Lance's mother said, holding up the empty basket as if to offer proof. "Do you have more?"

Julia walked to the warming drawer, took the basket, and began refilling it with warm rolls as the mother stood behind her, scrutinizing every inch of the kitchen much like Julia's own mother would have done—only bitchier.

"You made all this?" Donna asked, gesturing to the mountains of food that, according to Lance's family, was unfit to serve. All if it growing cold, discarded, worthless.

Julia surmised that she was probably getting ready to hear a lecture about hormones, preservatives, or starving children in the third world, so she snapped, "Yes!"—no longer in the mood for gentle formalities.

"All of it?" Donna asked as if she didn't believe it. *"Yourself?"*

"Yes! I baked the bread. I cooked the meat—I didn't kill the turkey, but I would have if I'd had to. Do you have a problem with that?"

"No," the woman said. "Actually, I'm impressed." She surveyed the kitchen again. "You don't have a staff?"

"No," Julia snapped then laughed a little at the absurdity.

"But how did you plan on keeping this place without a staff?"

"*I* didn't plan on keeping this place—it's Lance's place. I don't live here. I know it may not appear that way, but I've got a home of my own," she said as if she'd only suddenly remembered her small farmhouse in Oklahoma. "I didn't even know Lance had bought this place until . . ." She thought back on it with a sad, mournful regret. "Until I saw him on the *Today* show."

Tears came then from a well so deep inside Julia that she hadn't even known it existed. "I hate this place," Julia said through clenched teeth, no longer seeing Lance's mother, no longer speaking to anyone or anything besides the walls that surrounded her.

It was something she'd never said or done, but the need had been there all along, gnawing at her. She'd thought it made her stronger, denying the urge to cry, to rage, to feel.

Giving in then felt like a loss and like a victory. She was slowly succumbing to the thought of being normal. She felt like maybe from that point on it wouldn't be so exhausting being her.

"Julia," Donna Collins said, "it's okay, dear. In fact, it's better than okay. I think you and I are going to get along just fine." Julia looked at the woman who calmly nodded as if to say that Julia hadn't misheard. "Lance has been almost off his tracks for a while now. And, sweetheart, today we saw the wreck." Then she glanced away. "I have a bit of a confession to make actually." She gestured at the opulent, cavernous rooms. "When he bought *this*, I thought you were to blame—I admit it. I thought you were pushing him off course, but honey I know now that you're the only thing that's been keeping him on."

"You mean," Julia said, hiccupping through her breaking throat, "I'm not a bad girlfriend?"

And then Donna Collins laughed, and Julia thought it was one of the most beautiful sounds she'd ever heard. Donna walked closer and enveloped her into a hug. "No, I couldn't have picked a better one."

Julia let herself sink into the sheer comfort of a mother's hug for a moment then pulled away to see Donna face to face. "I'm sorry I can't cook for vegetarians."

"That's okay, dear," the mother said softly. "You'll learn."

Julia pulled a paper towel off the roll and blew her nose.

She saw the feast that would go uneaten, realized how far she was from home. "My dad has six brothers and sisters," Julia said. "When we all get together, no one has a house big enough to hold us all so we spill out onto porches and into yards and people eat in every room in the house. And everyone brags on my mom's bread, and we all know not to eat anything my Aunt Beverly makes because she put my Uncle Horace in the hospital once." Julia looked up at Donna. "There was an unfortunate custard incident."

"Oh, I see." Donna laughed. "That sounds nice."

Julia rubbed her eyes and sighed. "It is."

"It sounds like where you belong."

Julia loved *Gone with the Wind*. She'd always thought the world would be a better place if there were more Melanies and fewer Scarletts—just as long as she got to be one of the Scarletts. And as she stood in Lance's kitchen, she saw Vivian Leigh's tearstained face, heard Clark Gable telling her that she drew her strength from the red earth of Tara. Then Julia thought about the plans she and Lance had made together in a garden that didn't yet exist. And she knew there were some places where some things can never grow.

"How do you know when love . . ." Julia felt the tears on her face. She heard her voice crack. "How do you know when love just isn't enough?"

"When he doesn't come after you."

Chapter Thirty

You can't hold on to everything. Some cards simply have to be discarded.

"Fancy seeing you here," Mac said when she sat down.

She shrugged. She looked around the empty café, but of course, he was talking to her. She wondered then if Mac had no family, or if he was like Julia—hiding. If he came there every day and dissolved into a world of his own making simply because he preferred that to reality.

"So, how's the love story going?"

She sipped a cup of tea, felt the warmth seep into her hands, almost burning, but she didn't pull away. She just stared at the steam that spiraled from the cup and said, "Love makes a terrible MacGuffin."

She glanced around, hoping to see her waitress-slash-therapist, but instead there was a man manning the cappuccino machines. He glanced at the TV behind the counter. He was either incredibly dedicated or a little sad to be there alone working on Thanksgiving Day. Then she remembered those long-ago, anonymous holidays in New York, and she didn't feel sorry for him anymore.

"Hey, you're a female," Mac said as if he'd just noticed.

"Yes," Julia said. "Yes, I am." She felt somehow re-assured that at least that much hadn't changed.

"Maybe you can help me. I think I need a female perspective," Mac said, spinning in his seat, resting his elbows on his knees. "I'm working on a futuristic war thriller—think *Casablanca* meets *Star Wars.*"

"*Okay . . .*" Julia tried, not sure if that was a combo she could really imagine since it was far from being the soup and sandwich of the movie world.

"So I've got my hero and my heroine and I want them to meet, but not like . . . you know . . . boring. Got any advice?"

Julia fingered her napkin. She thought back to another restaurant in another city in what seemed like another life.

"Maybe she's just sitting in a café," she said, almost to herself. She closed her eyes, heard a distant clattering of thunder, felt a damp breeze blow through the open door. "Maybe it's raining. Maybe that's why he walks in, or maybe he's meeting someone—maybe he lies and says he's meeting her. Maybe he just sits down at her table, and she knows—just knows somehow—that that's it. That all her life has led her to that table at that time and—"

But Mac cut her off before she could finish. "No." She opened her eyes and realized that she was three thousand miles away from her fantasy. That the fantasy was really, truly over.

Mac was shaking his head vigorously back and forth. "Who's gonna believe that? I mean—no offense—but that's just crazy."

"Yeah," Julia whispered. "I guess it is."

But Julia had to wonder. Was it really crazy? Or was love just that easy? She thought for the first time in her life that maybe finding love was as simple as saying yes when it asks to sit down at your table. Nina found it when she was seven. Caroline found it at twenty-two. Her mom and dad had had it for more than forty years—and that, she knew, was the miracle.

Finding love is easy—it's keeping love that's hard.

The café was quiet for a long time. On the TV someone kicked a field goal, but the man behind the counter acted like he didn't care. Mac went back to his stalled story, and Julia just sat staring, finally understanding why she couldn't write a happy ending, knowing that endings are—by definition—always a little bit sad.

"Hey, you maybe wanna go get coffee or something sometime?" Mac said after a while, and Julia jumped.

She glanced around the empty room, double-checking that he really was talking to her. "Mac," she said slowly, "we're *in* a coffee house."

"Oh." He looked down then back at her. "You maybe wanna go someplace else sometime?"

"No. I don't think I can." She saw Pedro's cab appear through the long glass window. She stood and gathered her things. "But thanks for asking."

"Hey," Mac called as she walked away. "Do I know you?"

"No." She laid some money on the table and looked around the small café, seeing things the way you do when you know you'll never see them again. "No, Mac. I'm just a girl, looking for a happy ending."

She was already pushing through the door when she heard him ask the empty room, "Who's Mac?"

◆

"Where's Julia?" Lance asked. He looked around the kitchen, but it was empty. "What? Is she upstairs?" He started for the foyer, but he wasn't worried—not until he saw his mother's face. "Mom, what's going—"

"She left, Lance. She's going to call you later, but she couldn't stay."

"Mom, that's crazy. Where—"

"She couldn't stay, darling." Then Donna composed herself. She stood up straight, and Lance remembered that his mother was a tall woman, a stately woman. "She needed to leave."

"Leave and go . . ." But Lance didn't finish. He already

knew the answer. In a flash he was darting for the door, reaching for his keys.

"Lance, come back here." It wasn't a request.

Lance spun on her. "I *knew* you'd do this!" he snapped. "You had to run her off. You had to hate her based on principle. You don't know her!"

"Actually . . ." He heard the faintest sound of emotion in her voice. "I think I know her pretty well."

"Where did she—" Lance started, but was cut off when his mother called into the dining room, "Bob, dear, would you come here a second?"

"Mom!" Lance tossed his head side to side. "Mom, just tell me how long ago she—"

"Yes, dear?" Bob said, appearing at his former wife's side.

"I was just getting ready to tell our son he's being a horse's ass and I thought you might want to join me."

♠

"Amanda?" Julia asked.

"Oh, my gosh, Julia! Where are you? Things are crazy here. First, Lance was all like 'where's Julia' and then his mom was all 'she left' and then . . . long-story-short . . . intercom system."

Julia leaned against the bank of pay phones. She had her

purse but not her cell phone. And yet she had remembered to pack six pairs of tube socks, a hairdryer, and Nina's deodorant—so no matter what happened, she was going to be blown-dry and perspiration-free. It was a start.

"Amanda, can I talk to—"

But there was no need to finish the sentence, because just then she heard Caroline take the phone and yell, "Where are you?"

"I'm at the airport, Caroline."

"The airport?" Caroline shouted. "Julia, what—"

"I'll get Lance," Nina said, but Julia shouted, "No!"

From her bank of pay phones she could see a family waiting by the gate.

"No," she said, softer this time. "I don't want to talk to Lance. I don't want to do—you know, what has to be done—over the phone. I'll . . ." She called upon her inner Scarlett. "I'll think about that tomorrow."

"Well, it's probably a good thing," Caroline said, "because when you disappeared, Lance and his parents went into the den and closed the door and they've been screaming bloody murder ever since."

"Except when it's quiet," Nina added. "It's scary when it's quiet."

There was a long pause before Caroline said, "You're not someone who runs, Jules. You're not someone who quits."

"I know, Caroline. I know who I have been, and I know who I've been trying to be and—"

"You gave too much." It was Nina. Her voice was calm and clear, and she spoke in the way of someone who has no doubt—the way of someone who had been there. "You can't do everything, Jules. It's okay if you want to go home."

Julia realized then how easy it would have been for Jason to make Nina happy. Ridiculously easy. It was both a blessing and a curse, low expectations. Jason didn't have to meet her halfway, not even close. Julia wondered in that moment if all relationships are like that—someone giving more, someone giving less. She thought of what she'd given up for Lance, but then she stopped herself. She didn't want a score card. She didn't want to be that girl.

And then she thought about Nina, and *The Checks,* and she finally understood that Nina had grown tired of meeting Jason more than halfway, and now she was going to get Jason's fifty percent any way she could, one month at a time.

Behind her, in the still, empty terminal, someone announced a flight to Dallas, and Julia knew it was time to leave L.A.—to cut the cards anew and shuffle.

"So let me see if I've got this," Lance said, gearing up to reel off the facts that he'd heard before, facts burned into him, dates and places and pieces of logic that never changed and never mattered. There wasn't anything new—there never was. There are no new stories—Shakespeare got them all. "So one day when I'm seven—"

"Your father and I decided he should leave."

How can she do that? he wondered. *How can she be so calm?* She could just as easily have been saying, *We decided to paint the house blue,* or *We took a vacation to Mexico.* But no. She was talking about the most important decision of his life as if it was as trivial as deciding what to make for dinner.

"We wanted you to have a normal childhood. It wasn't fair to drag you all over the world. We wanted you in schools. I wanted to keep working, and . . . most importantly . . . we wanted to be able to be in a room together twenty-five years later and not hate what we'd become."

"Whatever." He shook his head. He was too tired to deny it anymore. He tried to go toward the door, but then he saw his dad, who had been there all along—quietly watching—and Lance knew that moment was just like all the others. Robert Wells was there, in the shadows, a part of their little family that could never be completely cast away.

"What I just want to know . . ." Lance started. He stared at his father—it was like staring at himself. "What I want to know is when we became not good enough for you."

He'd spent his whole life thinking it, but Lance didn't think he'd ever said it before, and once the words were free, he wanted to shove them back in. He wanted to be cool again, angry, or indifferent. The last thing in the world he wanted was to care.

"Never," the father said.

"Okay. Whatever. I'm out of here."

"Son, wait," Robert tried, reaching out for Lance. "The truth is, I want to make up for that now. I want to spend time with you. I want to get to know you."

"Yeah," Lance scoffed, "but I'm *working*. Does that sound familiar?"

"Fine." Bob threw his hands up in defeat. "Let's work together. Let's do something we can both be proud of. Let's—"

"You don't want to be in a movie with me, Dad," Lance bit back. "You want to be in a *hit*." He inched closer to his father, watched him flinch. "How long has it been? That Oscar's got to be getting kinda dusty."

When Robert backed away, his gaze fell. When he spoke, his voice was soft. "For someone who hates me so much, you're doing your best to act like me."

Lance didn't realize how long he stood there. He felt a weight on his arm, heard his mother's voice, "What do you *want*, Lance?" Donna asked. "Don't ever get so caught up in what you can have that you lose sight of what you want."

But Bob had walked away. He sat down at the game table and started shuffling cards—a practiced gesture, strong and sure. "What's it gonna be, son? Are you in or are you out?"

Chapter Thirty-one

If the cards are still on the table, the score may be recalculated. But once the cards have been mingled, the score stands.

M om?" Julia said.

"Daddy's already on his way, sweetheart. Caroline called us. He'll meet your flight and take you home."

Home. Julia didn't know whether it was exhaustion or her mother's voice or the word itself that made her start to cry right there in the middle of the Dallas/Fort Worth Airport.

"Things will work out, sweetheart. They always do." Julia nodded, rubbed her eyes, tried to believe it. "Well, just look at Steve and Caroline."

And then Julia's tears stopped. She hiccupped. "What about Steve and Caroline?"

"Didn't you see him?"

"See who?"

"Steve!" her mother said, running out of patience. "He left the kids with us and flew out to get Caroline. He's taking her to Hawaii for three days. They're leaving tomorrow."

"Wow," Julia said, knowing Caroline in California would probably pale in comparison to Caroline in Hawaii. "That's good news."

"I should say so. I don't think those children have a stitch of clothes that haven't been bleached or shrunk. He couldn't afford for her to stay gone any longer."

What was so sad about that, Julia didn't know, but somehow she burst into tears again—uncontrollable tears.

"Oh, honey," her mother said. "Julia, it's gonna be okay. It's not as bad as you think, sweetheart. I know these last few months have been hard on you, but you'll be okay. I know you, darling. You always end up okay."

And then Julia stopped. *You always end up okay.* Was that a prophecy or just an observation from the woman who knew her best? Julia didn't know and didn't care. She only knew that it was true. She had survived worse and for far longer. All she had to do was think of Harvey and remember how strong a broken heart can be.

"Yeah," she said, her voice scratchy but growing stronger. "It'll be good to be home. I have work to do."

She waited for an *I told you so* even though her mother

hadn't technically said a word to that effect. When it didn't come, Julia breathed deeper. She felt stronger. She knew the way home from there—the card that should come next—and she had just found the strength to play it when she heard her mother say, "You know, Lance is just like your father."

When Julia walked into the cold, dark house, she didn't recognize it. It was just as well. She'd become a person she didn't recognize. She wanted her old bed, her old sheets, and maybe when she woke up, she'd be back in her old life.

Her bag hung from her shoulder, but she didn't think about where she'd been. When thoughts tried to fight their way to the front of her mind, she'd block them out, and so they lagged there, lingering like a piece of a photograph that had been cut out and tossed aside. Julia didn't allow herself to think about the rest of the picture.

She reached for the switch inside the door, knowing exactly where she'd find it. She turned on the light and started for the stairs, but before she reached the landing, someone said, " 'Bout time you got home."

Julia froze, unable to step or turn.

Lance was lying on the sofa, squinting his eyes against the light.

"How did you—"

"Private plane," he said before she could finish.

"Oh." Then she realized she was shifting, she was nervous, she was about to be sick.

"You left," he said, but there wasn't a threat in his tone, no accusation. It was as if all his anger was spent and he didn't have the energy to muster a good fight.

"Yeah," she said. "I did." She shifted again, then said, "Lance, don't . . ." She started, but he gestured for her to stop. It was a cool gesture. Maybe, she thought, they would just go back to being friends. But they had never been friends. Not really.

"You left before the fun started."

"I know. I'm sorry. I—"

"I'm doing that movie with my dad."

Shock passed through her, then relief. "I'm glad," she said finally. "I think that's great."

He nodded slowly—not really agreeing, but trying to. "I know why you left, Julia. It was probably the right call." He straightened on the couch then stood. "We both know now that it probably was a mistake for you to come there," he said, and her tears started again, softly, gently; they told her that it was really over. She'd never been a failure—not by most definitions of the word, but she had failed at this.

Then Lance stepped closer and said, "I should have come here."

She tried to process what it meant, what he was saying, but her mind couldn't work that fast. He stepped closer.

"My house is going on the market on Monday. I'd make you a real good deal on it."

"Don't be silly, Lance."

"Who's being silly? I realized something today, Julia. I realized exactly how different from my dad I really am. I could walk away from it—I could. I'd work construction. I'd teach theater at the junior college. I'd—"

"No, Lance." He reached for her, but she pulled away. "Nina said something before I left. She reminded me that this stuff—this love stuff—it's supposed to be fifty-fifty." Words had never been so hard for her. "I don't want to give more than half; and I don't want to take more than half; and most importantly, I don't want to keep score."

He stepped closer. He said, "No scorecards."

"And I don't want to have to be a different person; and I don't want you to be a different person; and I don't want us to change each other into people we hate."

"No games." He waited for a long time, for her next protest, but it didn't come, so he said, "You keep running off and leaving these."

She saw her old box of cards in his hands, and without ceremony, he tossed it to her. "I made you a promise last spring, and I didn't keep my end of our bargain," he said. "That changes now."

The box felt light in her hands, uneasy.

He shook his head side to side, a gesture of surrender.

"You're a solitaire girl, Julia. So why don't you try that one on for size?"

She tore back the cardboard lip of the box and turned it upright as the most beautiful ring she'd ever seen tumbled onto her palm. "Julia," he said simply, "will you play gin with me . . . forever?"

But Julia didn't say yes. Or no. She just stared at the glistening ring. And despite everything, she really, really wanted to see if it would fit.

"What if we don't make it?"

He looked at her. "What if we don't try?"

There was some crying. There was some hugging. And then finally there was a long, sweet kiss. When it was over, she heard Lance's last confession.

"Oh, one more thing you should probably know . . . my family is all coming here for Christmas."

Epilogue

From *Learning to Play Gin* by Julia James

There are no happy endings. An ending is, by definition, at least a little bit sad. But I don't blame Snow White and Cinderella for this delusion—who could? They didn't know when the story ended what life was going to be like afterward—that sometimes finding a prince is only the beginning of the story—and if you're lucky—the story will never end.

I could have walked away, and I almost did. But what they don't tell you in fairy tales, in the world of make-believe, is that I'm pretty sure it's not the last time I'm going to feel that way. I'll probably feel it a thousand more times. A thousand and one.

I sat down at this table knowing what the game was, knowing it might take me a while to learn it and that there would be no cheating anymore. But what I just now learned is that if you care enough about the person sitting across from you, you can forget about the winning and the losing hands.

You stop keeping score.

And you shuffle a little longer, and deal a little slower. Anything to make it last.